A Home for CHRISTMAS

A Short Story Collection

MK McClintock

Trappers Peak Publishing

TP

Montana

A Home for Christmas, and the stories contained within, is a work of fiction. Names, characters, places, and incidents either are the product of the author's imagination or are used fictitiously. Any resemblance to actual persons, living or dead, events or locales is entirely coincidental.

Trappers Peak Publishing

Published in the United States of America

McClintock, MK
A Home for Christmas; short stories/MK McClintock
ISBN-10: 0-991330641
ISBN-13: 978-0991330645

Cover design, formatting, and beta reading by Potterton House Author Services. Exterior mages Purchased RF from Dreamstime.

Edited by: Magnifico Manuscripts, LLC

PRINTED IN THE UNITED STATES OF AMERICA

For Lily.
Welcome to the family.

AUTHOR'S NOTE

Christmas in nineteenth-century America must have been a truly delightful occasion. Throughout my research, I came across customs and stories that not only delighted and entertained, but also gave me pause.

Settlers and explorers of the west often spent the holiday on wagon trains, or camped along an icy river, with only an outdoor fire to offer warmth. Some were families at sea who enjoyed dainty meals of roast fowl, plum pudding, fruits, and cider. Others were soldiers in Colorado, short on rations, who found a way to celebrate when their hunting party shot eight buffalo. Others still enjoyed the comforts of a warm cabin or fine house, with all the trappings and trimmings Christmas offered.

No matter how you spend the holiday, I wish you a special day surrounded by family or friends, good health, and much happiness.

-MK

Christmas Mountain

A Short Story

Copper Point, Montana Territory—December 1879

The evergreen left a trail of needles in the snow, and the cold filled August's lungs, but he didn't mind. Life outside the four walls of his cabin or clinic brought him great joy. Almost as much happiness as his daughter, Sarah. She trudged alongside him over the mountain, humming "O Christmas Tree" while Crockett, the dog they had rescued three winters ago, sniffed the surrounding trees. Soft flakes floated around them, their path to earth slowing as they passed through or landed on the low-hanging branches of the tall pines.

August caught the scent of smoke from the fire, left burning low at the cabin, and quickened his pace in anticipation of a hot cup of coffee. His daughter's sweet music stopped filling the air, and the dog raced into the trees, his wild barks alerting August that something was wrong.

Sarah's eyes opened wide and she ran after Crockett, disappearing behind a boulder that stood half again her size.

"Sarah, wait!" August dropped the rope securing the tree to his shoulder and raced toward his daughter as the dog's barks quieted. When August caught up with Sarah and the dog, it was the soft form huddled against the rock that drew his attention.

"Stand back." He knelt on the snow and pulled a thick scarf away from the almost frozen figure's face. Crockett nudged the stranger's arm. "Hold onto Crockett."

"Is she alive?"

August set his hand in front of the woman's mouth, the faintest hint of warmth released from her lips. "She's alive, but not for long if we don't get her inside." He lifted her carefully into his arms. Movement in the trees brought him around, and Crockett's low growl stopped as quickly as it had begun.

"A horse, Pa!"

August nodded. "One that had sense to find shelter in the trees. Can you help me and care for the horse?"

"Yes." His daughter moved with slow and confident steps toward the mare. She stopped almost two feet away, holding out her hand. The horse hesitated but then closed the distance and pressed its nose against Sarah's hand even as the young girl reached for the reins. She patted the horse, gently smoothing her hand over its mane. Father, daughter, horse, dog, and stranger made their way up the gradual slope to the front porch of the rough-hewn cabin.

"Please get the mare settled into the barn, and take Crockett with you."

His daughter acknowledged and led the animal away toward the shelter of the large barn. He carefully adjusted the woman in his arms to open the door and kicked it shut behind him. Inside, the embers continued to burn in the stone fireplace, heating the cozy room.

August walked through the main room and into his bedroom where he gently laid the stranger on his bed. After removing his coat and hat, he washed his hands and set about removing her outer clothing.

A soft knock diverted his attention to the doorway where Sarah stood, her apprehension evident.

"Please fetch me some warm water and clean cloths."

"Yes, Pa!"

August heard the hall cupboard open and close, but his eyes remained focused on his new patient. Her pale skin, smooth hands, and once fine clothing, gave her away as a lady of some breeding. He couldn't imagine what would drive anyone like her to his mountain, especially in this weather.

His daughter returned and asked, "Is she going to be all right?"

"I hope so." Although he didn't know what he would find once he examined the lady, he predicted it would be a long night. "It will be dark soon, and you have your school assignment to finish before tomorrow."

"But I want to help."

"I know you do, my darling, but do you remember what I told you?"

"A doctor must be educated."

He smiled. "That's right. Now go and finish your assignment and then we can have our supper."

"May I help after my schoolwork?"

"You may. Please, heat some broth and put the kettle on for tea. When she wakes, she'll need something warm inside of her."

Seemingly content with the compromise, Sarah left the room, closing the door behind her. August turned to the patient, brushing her fallen hair aside. Startled at what was revealed, his stomach clenched. She bore a striking resemblance to someone he once knew. With gentle care, he removed her dress and underclothes, careful to cover her and readjust the blanket as he examined her for any injuries, but he found only scratches and a large bruise on her hip. With her weak pulse and shallow breathing, his greatest concern now was hypothermia.

He washed her face, arms, and lower half of her legs before covering her back up with the heavy quilt—the last quilt his wife had ever made before she died. The woman shifted and moaned softly. August watched her lips try to move, but she couldn't manage more than a few shivers.

"Clara?"

Her hoarse words caused August to stiffen. He reached out and placed his hand flat against her brow. "Can you hear me, miss?"

Her eyelids fluttered and then closed. August thought she might doze off, but then she looked at him, and he stared into the bluest eyes he'd ever seen—a deeper blue than even his wife's.

"Clara?" Her voice sounded low and hoarse.

"She's not here." August brought the quilt up to her chin and pulled a chair closer to the bed. "Do you know what's happened?" He watched her confusion turn to fear. "I'm not going to hurt you. My daughter and I found you in the woods. You nearly froze."

She blinked a few times as though to clear her vision and seemed to relax. "May I have some water?"

August filled a glass from the pitcher he kept beside his bed and lifted her head while she slowly took several sips.

"Where am I?"

"You're in my cabin near the base of Shelter Mountain. Do you remember how you got here?"

She nodded and tried to sit up. August reached forward

and helped her until she leaned back against the plump pillows.

"Where are my clothes?"

"They're here but wet. You were unconscious, and I had to check for injuries."

She pulled the quilt up until nothing was exposed below her chin. "I'm sore but otherwise feel unharmed."

"Did you fall? You have a rather large bruise."

"I wounded my pride more than my body. Yes, I fell off my horse. My sister did not warn me about the steep terrain of your mountain."

August sat back. "Clara. You're Clarissa's sister? Katherine."

"Yes." She indicated her pile of clothes. "There's a letter from her in the pocket of my coat."

August rummaged through the clothes until he found the letter, folded and damp. He removed the single sheet of paper and stared down at his wife's delicate lettering. He lowered himself back into the chair and looked at Katherine.

"Clara never told me that she wrote to you." He glanced back down at the letter. "When did you receive this?"

"Last month."

August stared at her in disbelief. "How is that possible? Clara died four years ago."

A few tears fell from Katherine's eyes. "I know, and I am so sorry."

The gentle knock at the bedroom door reminded August that his daughter was to bring in soup and tea. He opened the door and lifted the tray from her hands before she peeked around him. A child with a natural exuberance for life and people, Sarah walked beside him to the bed, followed closely by the dog.

Sarah smiled, her eyes brightening. "Papa, she looks likes

Ma!"

Katherine and Sarah both looked to him. He set the tray beside Katherine on the bed and lifted his daughter onto his lap. "Sarah, I would like to introduce you to your aunt Katherine. She's your mother's sister."

Convincing Sarah to go to bed after she learned that Katherine was her aunt had not been an easy feat. Katherine, despite her weakened state, visited with Sarah, talking a little about Clara. Once she became too weary to continue, she promised Sarah to spend as much time with her as she wanted.

The next morning, along with Crockett, August trudged outside and down the slope to fetch the tree he and Sarah had picked out yesterday. Once inside, he stood the tree in the crock and secured the base with rocks. Christmas was his wife's most treasured holiday, and he swore that he would always carry on those traditions for his daughter.

He knelt down on the rug to lay a large strip of canvas at the base of the tree. Crockett sensed the presence in the room before August and left his space on the rug. August glanced up and saw Katherine leaning against the door frame, rushed to her side, and set his arm around her waist.

"You're not strong enough to be up."

"My legs work just fine, but it seems I need a little help." She pointed to the main room. "May we go in there? I don't wish to sleep right now."

He hesitated for a few seconds, and instead of helping her walk, he gently lifted her into his arms, surprising Katherine, and carried her into the room where he set her on an overstuffed chair in front of the fire. He took the wool blanket from the back of the chair, wrapping it around her, and then opened the front door when Crockett scratched to go out.

"Is he safe out there by himself?"

Smiling, August said, "He knows what he's doing."

"Unlike me."

August smiled and studied the delicate features so much like his wife's.

"You could have sent word that you were coming. I would have met you at the train depot in Helena." He settled into the chair opposite her. "How did you manage to get from there to here?"

Katherine's cheeks brightened to a lovely shade of pink. "I hired a driver, but he never showed up, so I bought the horse."

August grinned. "I met the horse."

"I feel so foolish coming the way I did, unannounced. I wasn't sure you'd want to see me, but I had to come for Clara."

August's disposition sobered. He had made a lot of promises to Clara before she died—among them an eastern education and respectable marriage for Sarah. Clara had not asked a lot of him, but shared with him her hopes and dreams for their daughter one day meeting her family, but never once before her passing, did she mention writing the letter to Katherine.

"Why did you only receive the letter last month? Four years is a long time for it to be lost." August stood and walked to the door. Crockett sauntered inside, covered with fresh snow, and after a quick shake, he settled on the rug next to Katherine's feet. August carried a cloth over and knelt beside the dog to rub him down, all the while mindful of Katherine's eyes on him.

"What did my sister tell you of our father?"

August settled back into his chair. "She wouldn't talk about him. When we first married, she only said her family wouldn't be at the wedding."

"I wanted to be there, and I've never been more sorry that I didn't attend. Clara always wanted a quiet life as a teacher and a mother, and coming west was the only place she believed she could find both."

"It doesn't sound like a bad way to live."

"It wasn't, but my father had other plans for his daughters. When Clara heard that school teachers were needed in small towns out west, she didn't hesitate. She picked a place on the map, found a position, and this is where she ended up."

"Did you disagree with her decision?"

"I admired her for standing up for her convictions and to our father. His plans for us were to marry and have our husbands work in his import business. What Clara never understood was although I didn't wish to marry someone who desired only my father's money, I did want to continue helping with the company. I had a knack for business, and I enjoyed the work."

August reached down and rubbed Crockett's ears when the dog moved to settle beside his chair. "Clara didn't know. She always thought you'd chosen your father's path instead of your own."

"I did choose my father's path, but it was my choice and it's what I wanted, much like Clara made her choice to venture west."

August watched as Katherine pulled the blanket up and around her shoulders and stared into the fire. The glow from the flames lightened the tips of her loose hair, and he turned away.

Katherine continued. "After our father died, I realized how my choice, however safe, caused me to miss so much by staying home. I envied Clara's adventurous spirit."

August made himself busy by adding another log to the

fire. "It's not all adventure. Life is hard out here, and rewarding. I don't believe your sister ever regretted her choice to come west or marrying a country doctor. Naturally, there were times when she longed for the conveniences and comforts of the city."

Katherine leaned forward in the chair, and August watched her thick, raven locks cascade over her shoulders.

"Clara never wrote that she missed home. Quite the opposite."

August smiled. "She wouldn't have said anything. I wish I had known that she wrote to you. I would have brought Sarah to visit and given her a chance to know her grandparents."

Katherine settled deeper into the chair. "I found Clara's letter among my father's papers after he passed. I know he was disappointed that Clara left, but more than that, I do believe he missed her. I couldn't tell you why he took the letter, but I do know that Clara's death left a hollowness inside of him. I saw it in his eyes whenever I spoke of her." She smiled. "My father would have liked Sarah, and enjoyed being a grandfather."

"Clara and I discussed returning east after Sarah was born, debating that there are far more opportunities for a surgeon back home than here and more educational and social opportunities for Sarah. Clara spoke of returning more and more near the end, not only for Sarah but for herself. I feel she missed her family."

"And you didn't want to leave?"

August shook his head and returned to his chair. "I left Boston because I wanted a different kind of life. I would have given Clara anything, and I almost agreed, but I couldn't leave the people who depended upon me, my practice. It was selfish of me."

"No, it wasn't."

August raised his head until his eyes met hers. "I knew her time was near an end. I didn't leave the cabin much during those last days, but a young boy from town fell from the roof of his barn. There wasn't anyone . . . I couldn't not go." August looked away. "Clara was dead when I returned home the next morning."

The next day, Katherine stood on the front porch and breathed in fresh morning air, pulling the edges of the blanket closer to her body. The chill from the early winter breeze comforted her in a way she didn't expect. The piercing cold filled her lungs, and the deeper she breathed, the stronger and more clearheaded she felt. She'd gone to bed the night before with more questions than answers after her conversation with August. Katherine knew her sister better than anyone else before Clara came out west. They had been best friends, childhood playmates, giggling school girls, and finally grown women who had chosen different paths.

A faint howl ricocheted off the mountain and disappeared into the thick forest. August's cabin stood high enough on the slope to glimpse the small town below through the trees. Katherine wondered what type of person chose to live a life of such isolation and hardship, and yet, she envied those strong enough to take the risk.

"Aunt Katherine, I know I already said this, but you look a lot like my ma."

Katherine started at the quiet voice from behind. She turned around to see Sarah standing just outside the front door. "Well, good morning, Sarah. So do you. You have her eyes and lovely nose, but I think you have your father's smile."

Sarah beamed at the comparison and stepped forward,

joining Katherine at the deck railing. Unlike Katherine, the young girl seemed unaffected by the cold. "She didn't like to talk about you."

Surprised, Katherine looked down at her niece. "What do you mean?"

"It made her cry. I think she missed you."

"I missed her, too." Katherine watched a small group of deer move deftly through the trees. "But she got to live here in this magical place with you and your father."

"I know Ma loved us, but I think maybe she would have been happier at home with you and her ma and pa."

Katherine knelt on the porch in front of Sarah, ignoring the cold seeping through her skirts. "I happen to know that your mother wouldn't have been happy anywhere else but here. You see, sometimes a person longs for something different, for an adventure. Clara loved adventures, but she loved you more."

Sarah's beautiful brown eyes met Katherine's, and it was like looking into a younger version of Clara.

"You really think so?"

"I know so. She told me in her letters." Katherine stood and brushed off her skirts. "Now, why don't we fix breakfast and then you can show me where you keep your tree decorations."

"You're staying for Christmas?"

"Of course I am." Katherine draped an arm over Sarah's shoulders and led her back into the house. It had been a challenge getting here, and she wasn't leaving before she had a chance to spend the holiday with her sister's family. Crockett met them on the other side of the door, eager to be let out. She watched the dog race over the porch and into the snow, barking as he ran in the direction of the deer.

"Why did you name your dog Crockett?"

Sarah grinned. "Pa reads to me at night and the story about Davy Crockett is one of my favorites. Do you like dogs?"

Katherine laughed at the excited barks coming from outside. "I've never had one of my own, but I do like your dog."

They walked companionably inside where the fire burned hot and warmed the interior of the cabin. The scent of coffee wafted tantalizingly toward Katherine and she realized the source when August walked in from the kitchen. "I thought perhaps Sarah and I could decorate the tree, or we could all decorate it together."

"It's a good idea." August handed Katherine a hot cup of the coffee. Her hands circled the creamware mug, and August spared a moment to watch her blow the steam gently away before sipping. "How about it Sarah? Only three days left until Christmas."

Sarah scooted away. "But we decorate the day before Christmas."

"That's right." August lowered himself until he was eye level with his daughter. "Why don't we try something different this year? We can go down the mountain and help light the candles on the tree. You could see some of your friends, and then tonight we will decorate our tree."

Katherine enjoyed the shifting expressions on the young girl's face—just like her mother. Clara's moods used to alter quicker than they could untie their shoes and soak their feet in the warm sand on a summer day at the beach. The little things about her sister were what she missed most. She brought her thoughts back to Sarah, whose face donned a big smile.

"Okay, Pa. We can decorate early this year."

Sarah spoke with such definite authority, leaving Katherine to wonder how often August managed to resist the gentle requests and demands of his daughter. Katherine wanted to laugh, and it looked to her that August would join her, but instead he agreed and stood.

"I'll bring the box in from the barn, and while I'm gone, you can show Katherine the angel you made this year. Come to think of it, I haven't seen it yet. You must have hidden it to perhaps surprise me on Christmas Eve?" August grinned and opened the front door to collect the box, leaving Katherine alone with her niece.

"I can't wait to see this angel you made for the tree." Katherine's own smile faded when she saw the gentle shrug and bright eyes. "Sarah, what's wrong?"

"I didn't make a new angel."

Katherine settled down in the rocking chair and held out her arms. Sarah closed the distance in a few steps and allowed Katherine to lift her onto the chair. "Do you have an old angel?" Katherine asked.

"Pa said we should make a new angel this year for new memories, but I like the old angel."

Katherine swept the girl's hair out of her eyes. "Did your mother make the old angel?"

Sarah's head bobbed gently up and down. "I don't want Pa to be sad."

Katherine gently pulled Sarah toward her and enveloped the young girl within the circle of her arms. "He might be a little sad, but I promise he wants you to be happy. If you want to use your mother's angel, I'm sure he'll be okay."

Sarah lifted her head and looked at her. "You think so?"

"I do." She helped Sarah down, urging her along.

With a smile and clear eyes, Sarah dashed off in search of her mother's Christmas angel.

August hefted the crate of carefully packed glass ornaments and ribbons, a collection his wife had brought with her from Boston. The short white candles reserved for the holidays were wrapped in brown paper, some more used than others. He remembered that Clara had made a small doll ornament for Sarah every year, giving it to their daughter as her first Christmas gift. They would gather around the hearth drinking hot chocolate and eating a slice of fruit cake. They'd followed that tradition with a walk in the snow if the wind wasn't blowing, and then return for breakfast and a day of reading, games, laughter, and of course, the Christmas dinner with all the fixings.

For August, the memories faded a little more with each passing year.

He walked the wooden steps up to the front porch. Crockett rushed past him, sat at the door, and thumped his tail, waiting. August laughed and reached for the door handle. It opened before he had the chance to grasp it. Katherine stood on the other side, her smile a bright reminder of something that had been missing from this home and their lives.

"That looks heavy." Katherine stepped aside to allow him and Crockett to pass. "I was just about to go and help Sarah look for the angel."

August set the crate down beside the evergreen and removed his coat. "She's lost it already?"

"She's looking for her mother's old angel."

August dropped his coat on one of the hooks by the door and slowly turned. Katherine watched the confusion and hurt shadow his eyes and wished she could ease some of the suffering he and Sarah still carried.

"I know I don't have the right to offer your daughter advice, but Sarah confessed that she really wants to use her mother's angel this year. She said they made it together the last Christmas Clara was alive. She misses her, just as you do."

August glanced up to the second level of the cabin where he kept a trunk of Clara's belongings, items he cared for too much to give away. He knew the angel was at the bottom of the trunk, wrapped in one of his wife's old shawls. He knew because that's where he put it the week after she died. The week after their last Christmas together.

Katherine continued. "It doesn't hurt for her or you to hold onto something as precious as a Christmas angel. My memories of Clara are good ones, but old. I wish I had known her those last few years. I always believed I had time to visit, to send her one more letter, but I ran out of time. I came here because Clara asked me to, but that's not the only reason."

August watched Katherine prepare herself for whatever she was about to say. "I thought Clara was foolish to have left home. I admired her, certainly, but I believed she had made a mistake. Every time I did write, I told her about the wonderful things happening at home, asking her to come back and never asking about her life here. When I finally realized that she was happier here than she ever would have been in Boston, it was too late to mend the distance between us over the years. However, I would have loved to have tried. I was too stubborn to try and understand Clara's reasons for leaving."

August studied the slight shift of her body, and the deep rise and fall of her chest. The guilt she must have felt was evident in her misty eyes. "She never blamed you, not for any of it. In fact, she had—"

"I found it!" Sarah ran into the room, out of breath and beaming. Her smile faded when she realized August was in the room, and he quickly called her over, offering a smile of his own.

"I forgot how pretty she was." August lifted the angel from his daughter's hand. "She's perfect."

His eyes met Katherine's, and her tears fell when Sarah showed them the angel—a little piece of Clara, a cherished holiday memory. There was still more to be said, more stories to share and memories to relive, yet for now, he set aside any remnants of sadness to enjoy his daughter's joy.

The following morning, red and silver ribbons were intertwined with the green branches and glass balls. White candles covered strong branches while Sarah's homemade doll ornaments sat on others. They enjoyed decorating the tree last night after August took them down the mountain to light candles on the town's Christmas tree. It had been a new experience for Katherine, and a memory she would cherish.

Alone now, surrounded by a peace she rarely experienced, Katherine pet Crockett in front of the hearth. The fire flickered, causing the flames' shadows to dance over the log walls. The scent of yeast drifted from the rising loaves of bread waiting on the kitchen counter. Quiet surrounded Katherine and Crockett as they enjoyed a few moments alone before the others woke.

Katherine had awakened early that morning. At her parents' home in Boston, she rarely rose before a maid came in to draw back the curtains and bring her a cup of tea. Back home, from morning until night she rarely had a moment alone. Here, she enjoyed the solitude of August and Sarah's cabin—her sister's cabin.

Her eyes scanned the room, settling for a moment on each piece of furniture, blanket, and painting. She recognized two of the paintings as the wedding gifts her parents had sent Clara nearly a year after she wrote to tell them about her wedding.

Shock had swept through the family, and though Katherine would have wanted to be there for her sister's wedding, by the time she had convinced her parents not to be angry, Clara was already married. Having met August, Katherine knew they would have approved and welcomed him into the family, despite their initial misgivings. Clara had made a wise choice in a husband.

Footsteps in the hall indicated that her precious quiet was about to end. She did not mind and smiled up at August when he walked in.

"You're up early. Did you not sleep?"

"I did. Better than I have in a long while." Katherine rubbed behind Crockett's ears once more before she stood and walked toward the kitchen. She lifted the cloth from the loaves and checked the heat in the oven.

"You bake?"

"Not well, but our cook gave me a few lessons while I was still in school. I remember how to bake bread."

August leaned around her to look at the unbaked loaves. She closed her eyes for a second and enjoyed his masculine scent, then took one step back.

"They look good. I haven't mastered bread, but Sarah's getting pretty good at it. We generally purchase our bread from the local baker."

August leaned back against the wood counter, and Katherine sensed him watching her. She slid the loaves into the oven and glanced at the clock on the mantel to gauge the time before facing him. "When does Sarah normally wake?"

"Not for another hour or two."

Katherine leaned against the long table in the center of the kitchen. "I know my arrival was unexpected, and I want you to know that I don't anticipate encroaching on your hospitality for long, but I do hope you'll allow me to spend more time with Sarah, after the holidays."

"You're staying then?"

"In town. I hope to find a place for at least a month, perhaps longer." Katherine stepped closer to him, her hands bunching the towel she still held. "It's not only for Clara. I've missed so much, and with mother and father gone, you and Sarah are the only family I have left."

Katherine remained still when August closed the distance between them. He drew the towel away from her and gently lifted her hands. "I was angry with all of you for a long time. I didn't know you, but I thought you'd abandoned Clara because of her decision." He steadied his gaze on hers as Katherine waited. "I found another letter in her small desk. It was dated before we knew she was ill. She was reconsidering her return to Boston. She did love it here, but she felt that the opportunities available to Sarah in the East would give our daughter a better life. I didn't disagree, but she and I had a different view of life back home."

"You must have despised us."

August shook his head and brushed his fingers down her cheek. "I wanted to, but I was the one at fault. What I'm trying to say is that we are all any of us have left, and no matter what's happened, or what might have happened, I know Clara had enough love in her heart for everyone. She would have wanted you to stay. I want you to stay."

Katherine waited for the familiar well of tears to fall, then squeezed August's hand. "Thank you."

"I do insist on one thing."

"Anything."

"Stay here."

"I couldn't. I realize perception may be different out here, but . . ."

August laughed softly, and Katherine wasn't sure what to make of it. "There's a smaller cabin a short distance up the hill. It was the first one I built when I arrived. This one here I had built for Clara. I'm asking you to stay here in this house with Sarah. I'll sleep in the other cabin."

Katherine pulled away with some hesitation but managed to step back. "I don't know what to say."

"Say yes, or at least say you'll think about it."

"Sarah won't understand."

August contradicted her. "She will. I'll be here when I'm not sleeping or tending to patients in town. I promise there is nothing untoward about it, and this will give you time to know if you want to stay on a permanent basis."

Katherine knew what she wanted, or did she? Her plans had been temporary when she first boarded the train to come west. Katherine now longed for an adventure to look back on when she became a wife and mother—an experience she could call her own. Now that she was here, did she want to stay? Could she give up her life among Boston's elite to remain in Montana Territory where ball gowns were superfluous and wealth was often measured in quality rather than quantity?

Her father's lawyer, now hers, had assured her that the business would continue to run, but she should hurry back. A member of the family had always been at the helm of Donahue Imports. The clients and customers counted on the connection with Katherine, and she understood the importance of it. Her father had also understood, which is why he had groomed her to take over the company. Nevertheless, for a while longer at least, she would remain here and get to know August and Sarah.

Katherine knew he watched her when she walked from the

kitchen and into the large living area. The cabin was modest compared to her family's mansion in Beacon Hill or the home her parents had built, but never had a chance to enjoy, in Westbury, New York. Their family had enjoyed many happy years together. However, it was work and social obligations that occupied their lives and time. Such wealth was admirable, and yet in the end, Katherine had been left with things instead of family.

Her memories after Clara left had consisted of business meetings with clients rather than family dinners or decorating Christmas trees, the latter being left to the servants. The Donahue sisters had been loved deeply by their parents, but looking around, and now having met August and Sarah, Katherine understood why her sister had remained in Montana. August may believe that Clara wanted to return home, but Katherine couldn't imagine leaving a life like this behind, even if there was a letter. The majestic mountains, a simpler existence, and a life of substance, not of wealth. August and Clara had built their life on a foundation of love and hard work.

"Katherine?"

She turned at the sound of August's deep voice. He had followed her from the kitchen.

"I'll stay here, and I appreciate the offer for . . . time with Sarah."

"You're certain?"

She pondered his question, without having a definitive answer. This place where the mountains rose higher than the tallest buildings in Boston, or where the trees in the forests covered millions of acres—more land than she could ever walk upon in a lifetime. Montana wasn't her home, but it could be. It might be.

"I'm certain, but we should talk again. There are things . . ." Katherine glanced up to the second level where Sarah's peals of laughter and Crockett's excited barks filled the house.

"She'll be down any minute." August lowered his voice. "We'll talk more tonight, but for now I want to say thank you. This will mean the world to Sarah."

Only Sarah? Katherine wondered but left the thought to the silence. When Sarah climbed down the stairs while Crockett wagged his tail beside her, Katherine's heart filled with a curious sense of peace.

August observed Katherine and Sarah together throughout breakfast and morning chores. When he mentioned that they would be only an hour taking care of the animals and checking the buildings—something August tasked himself with daily—he was surprised when Katherine offered to help.

He doubted her abilities, though he didn't say as much to her. Instead, he found Clara's old work boots and coat and watched in amusement as Katherine slipped into both. Her long wool dress was too fine for the mountain, but she didn't seem to care. With a smile and an excited laugh, Sarah grasped Katherine's arm and pulled her outside, leaving August to follow behind.

August walked into the barn and nearly collided with Katherine. He reached out to stop her from tumbling forward. "The fun is inside."

"So Sarah said, but I've never touched one."

August shared a quick look with his daughter but neither managed to hide their merriment. "She won't hurt you, I promise." He held out his hand and was pleased when Katherine accepted. He guided her toward the short wooden stool beside the milking cow and urged her to sit down. "You don't have to do this."

"I want to, oddly enough."

She raised her eyes up, and August enjoyed a moment staring down at her. He knelt beside her and inched the stool forward. "Sarah, will you bring us that fresh bucket, please?" When the pail was set beneath the udders, August pointed to her hands. "You'll want to remove those."

Katherine looked down at her gloves, and August almost took pity on her. He didn't want to be cruel or make her feel inadequate. She said she would stay, and that pleased him more than he wanted to admit aloud. If she never worked a day during her time with them, he would still believe that he and Sarah were getting the better bargain.

"Can I show her?" Sarah stuck her head in between Katherine and August's shoulders.

"May I show her. Of course. You'll do a better job than me." August brought a second stool over. "Just watch out for—"

Frantic shouts from outside pressed August into immediate action. He rushed toward the door, but the young boy met him just outside the barn.

"Teddy. What are you doing up here?" August did a quick survey of the boy but saw nothing wrong with him.

"Doc Hollister, it's my little brother. He's awful sick and Ma's done all she can."

"Come inside—"

"I brought him here, Doc." Teddy hurried away, and August had no choice but to follow. He swore inside when he saw the horse and Teddy's brother slumped in the saddle. He rushed to the piebald, lifting the young boy from the saddle. In a few hurried, long strides, August had the boy inside the cabin and settled on his large bed. A minute later, the front door closed and Crockett was licking the young boy's face.

"Not now, Crockett."

Katherine stood beside the bed, her face rosy from the cold. "What do you need?"

August hid the grimace when he saw the gash on the boy's leg. "My medical bag is by the front door. Boil some water, gather clean cloths, and have Sarah add more wood to the fire."

August didn't wait or watch to see if Katherine did as he asked. His focus remained entirely on the boy. "Ollie, can you hear me, son?"

"He stopped talking on the way up here." Teddy walked into the room and stood close to his brother.

"What happened, and why did you bring him here? Your pa should have sent for me and taken him to the clinic."

Moisture filled Teddy's eyes before he caught his breath. "I think Pa's dead."

August stopped the process of removing Ollie's shirt and whipped his head around to look at Teddy. "How? When did this happen?"

"We were cutting a tree for firewood and it fell on our pa and Ollie. Ma tried to fix Ollie up, but she didn't know how. He wouldn't wake up. She stayed with Pa and sent me to you. It was closer."

"They're still in the woods?"

Teddy nodded, but his gaze never left his brother.

"I'll find your ma, but right now we have to take care of your brother. I need you to be strong for Ollie. Can you do that?"

Teddy raised his quivering chin, reminding August that he was only twelve.

"You did right bringing him here."

"Pa?"

August turned to see his daughter standing at the door. "Sarah, can you wait with Teddy by the fire and give him some of the bread Katherine made this morning?"

Sarah walked into the room and slipped her hand into Teddy's. August knew if someone could calm the boy it would be Sarah. Teddy hesitated to leave Ollie's side, but she whispered something that August didn't hear. A moment later, the children walked hand in hand from the bedroom, passing Katherine on the way. She set a bowl of water and stack of cloths on the table next to the bed along with his medical bag.

"The water hasn't boiled yet, but this is fresh."

"Can you help me?" August motioned her to the other side of the bed. "Wash his face and chest while I examine his leg. I need to be able to see if he has any other injuries."

Katherine did as he asked, quiet during her ministrations of the boy. August listened as she spoke softly to Ollie, and though he remained unconscious, his breathing calmed.

"Will he be all right?"

Katherine's soft inquiry was met with silence as August considered her question. Would he? August hoped, but couldn't know until the boy woke. The last time a person lay seriously ill in this bed was when Clara fought death. Patients rarely came to him because it meant going up the mountain, and few sick enough to need his services could make the short journey up the steep road. He originally chose this spot because of its seclusion, but if they'd lived closer to the small town and to his clinic, would Clara have lived? He asked himself that same question often, but his intellectual mind knew that nothing could have been done to save his wife.

"I hope so." August finished examining the boy after Katherine washed him and found two more small cuts in addition to the long gash on his leg. "He will likely remain unconscious while I stich his leg. Would you look in on Sarah and Teddy?"

"Of course."

August closed his eyes for a second when she walked passed him. A light rose scent wafted toward him, reminding him of his childhood home and some of his happiest memories. Every year since Sarah's birth, he planted a new rose, a feat that required time and dedication to get the plants rooted and healthy in this climate, but his mother had supplied him with grafts from her own prized gardens. Clara had never been one to tend the roses and had left their care to August. He and Sarah now tended them together, a task they both enjoyed.

August shook away the memories and listened to Katherine's light footsteps fade down the hall. He rummaged through his medical bag, pulling out the needle, thread, and bandages he would need to dress the wounds. Praying Ollie would remain unconscious, August poured alcohol over the needle, dabbed more on the wound, then meticulously threaded the gash closed.

Once the other cuts had been cleaned and salve applied, August checked his patient's temperature, relieved to find him only mildly warm. Katherine returned this time with a bowl of warm water and more cloths.

"How is he?"

"Better, I think, but we won't know until he wakes up." August accepted the water, soaked a cloth, and smoothed it over the boy's skin around his wound. Once he was confident he'd cleaned up every last bit of blood, he bandaged over the stitches, then washed his hands. "How are the children?"

"Strong. Sarah is amazing."

"She is." August stood and covered the boy with quilts. "I need to go and find their parents. Teddy thinks his father is dead and his mother stayed behind."

"Surely someone has found them by now."

August moved her into the hall and lowered his voice so as not to alert Teddy and Sarah of their conversation. "People who live outside of town can go days without seeing anyone. I need to find them, and Teddy will want to go, but . . ."

"You worry about what you might find?"

"It's colder than the night I found you outside."

"I'll be here with them, so you do what you must."

August looked toward the main living area where he heard the children's soft voices. "The year Clara died, I left two days before Christmas to tend to a patient."

"You've told me, and you did what you had to do."

"Yes, but I worry about Sarah. I don't want her to think . . . you'll talk to her? I know I don't have a right to ask, but I must leave shortly, and she won't understand."

Katherine's fingers brushed his arm where his shirt sleeve was still rolled up. "I will speak with her. She's strong and will be just fine."

Katherine stood behind Sarah and Teddy, an arm draped over each child. August said his good-byes, promising to return as soon as he could. When Teddy begged to go with him, August soothed the boy with logic.

"Ollie needs you here. When he wakes, he'll want family with him, and he'll be so happy to see you."

August received a reluctant nod from Teddy, kissed his daughter's cheek, and looked directly at Katherine. She wanted to go with him, to help him, to ensure he would return. It had not taken long for her to love this family. Not perhaps as Clara once had, but Katherine didn't have to wonder any longer what she missed by choosing a life of work over love.

"We'll be fine."

August told Crockett to stay when the dog started to follow him out the cabin, and then he was gone.

Katherine patted Sarah's shoulder and took a deep breath. "Sarah, will you help with supper? It's a little early, but it's been a long day. Teddy, would you like to sit with Ollie? We can eat in the bedroom, like a picnic."

Teddy first looked at her and then to her surprise at the Christmas tree. "Will Ollie get to see Christmas?"

Katherine held back the tears, drawing on the well-known Donahue strength to get her through this night. "We must believe that he will." She smoothed back Teddy's hair, much as her mother used to do with her as a child. "How about that picnic?"

They ate a meal of biscuits and cold meat from the larder. Katherine received her first cooking lesson from a child when Sarah showed her how to mix, roll, and shape the biscuits. She didn't have the heart to tell the child that she knew how to make the bread, for Sarah appeared to enjoy the task and the distraction.

The children sat on the edge of the bed—Teddy wanted to be close when Ollie woke—and Katherine occupied the chair while they ate mostly in silence. Darkness descended and Katherine experienced her first difficulty with the children when she told them it was time to sleep. Teddy finally agreed, but only because he was allowed to lie beside his brother. Sarah and Crockett laid down where Katherine slept to be close by in case Ollie stirred.

Katherine kept the fire fed and when she grew restless, paced in front of the small shelf of books. A familiar binding drew her notice. The written history of their family, one copy given to each daughter when they turned eighteen, appeared worn from many readings. Katherine carried it back to one of the chairs and slowly turned the pages. She'd not looked through her own copy in ages. Clara had added her own notes after she married and when Sarah was born. Sketches worthy of a talented artist graced some of the blank pages. Katherine stared at one of August and Sarah together on a horse.

"Clara, I'm so sorry." Katherine wiped at the tears and smoothed her fingers over the faces in the sketch. "You should be here with them. They miss you—I miss you. We missed so much, but I never once envied what you had until I came to your mountain." Katherine closed the book and leaned back, clutching it to her chest. With her thoughts on the children in the other room, and the man risking his life to save another, she stared into the flames and waited.

Her dreams were often vivid, but none so much as this. She wished to remain within the arms of Morpheus, and yet, the soft sound of her name spoken in a voice from the dream called on her to wake. Katherine slowly opened her eyes to see that at least one part of her dream was still real. When she saw the morning light touching the walls, she woke fully.

"I didn't mean to fall asleep. The children."

August knelt beside the chair and smiled, but Katherine now saw the weariness around his eyes. "The children are fine, and Ollie is awake. I believe he'll pull through."

Katherine smiled and tears of joy glistened in her eyes. She leaned forward and wrapped her arms around August before she fully realized what she was doing. When she did become aware of her actions, she didn't care. She pulled back to see a smile as big as her own.

August tucked a loose hair behind her ear. "Thank you for your help with the children."

"I wouldn't want to be anywhere else." Katherine realized it was true. The mansion in Boston and the sprawling estate in Westbury were part of a life slowly fading away. "Wait, what about their father? Was he . . ."

"No. Close, and he'll have a long recovery ahead of him, but he's alive."

"Thank God. Do they know?"

"I told Teddy already. The snow stopped during the night, and the road is passable enough to take the boys back to town in the wagon. I moved their father to my clinic, and they'll stay there together for a couple of weeks."

Katherine's eyes met his, searching for an answer she had yet to ask. "May Sarah and I go with you? I don't believe she'll want to be parted from you again, especially on Christmas Eve."

"I would like that."

August and Teddy readied the wagon while Katherine and Sarah packed a basket with meats and breads. Ollie wore one of August's shirts, cinched at the waist, and then was wrapped in extra blankets before August carried him to the wagon. Sarah insisted on riding in the back with the boys and Crockett, which left Katherine on the wagon seat with August, an arrangement August welcomed.

It wasn't only that she evoked pleasant memories of Clara, but more importantly, she reminded him that life always presented a person with second chances if they were willing to leap on faith and hope.

They ambled into the town of Copper Point, a well-established community consisting of two streets sided with an array of sturdy wooden buildings. August imagined families tucked away in their homes, close to the hearth and creating another season of memories. The clinic was the third largest building in town after the general story and livery. August had bought it from one of the first settlers of Copper Point when he left his lucrative practice back east to settle on the mountain. It stood as a point of pride to him and comfort to the town knowing he was there for them.

A young boy and his father had been saved, like many over the years, and August's family had grown at a time when he least expected. He didn't know what tomorrow or the days to come would bring, but he did know that his wife had sent Katherine to them at a time when Clara knew they would need her the most.

He settled Ollie on a cot in the recovery room with his father while Katherine and Sarah spoke with the boys' mother and offered her the basket of food.

"It's not much of a holiday meal, I'm afraid, but it's fresh and filling."

Samantha Collins shed tears in between her offering of thanks. "I have my family, and that's the only thing I could ever want. I thought I'd lost them. I don't know what I would have done had my Garrett and Ollie . . ."

August watched with pride as Katherine embraced the other woman. "I'll be back down tomorrow to check on you and change the bandages."

Samantha quickly shook her head. "It's Christmas. We'll be fine here. You've already done so much, and we can't . . . I can't ask for anything more."

To his surprise, Katherine spoke in his stead. "You're not asking. We'll all be here."

Samantha continued to cry even as she kissed her husband and hugged her sons.

August guided Katherine and Sarah from the clinic and

helped them into the wagon. This time Sarah sat between them, protected by their warmth. Crockett moved around in the back, content to watch the scenery and look out for people or animals.

The ride up the mountain was one of comfortable silence, and August wondered what thoughts occupied Katherine's mind. He was left wondering as he pulled up to the cabin and helped them down. Katherine and Sarah went into the house while he tended to the wagon and horses. Once the animals were tucked away in their stalls with fresh oats, he trudged toward the cabin.

On the front porch, he waited and listened. Sweet music sung by a voice too beautiful for description, drifted through the logs and into his heart. He gave into the moment and waited until Katherine finished before entering. Sarah leapt at him and wrapped her arms around his waist.

"Katherine said she'll help me make pies. You said we could have lots of pies this year, and maybe we can make extra and take some to Teddy and his family. Can we, Pa?"

August smiled down at his daughter, returning her hug. "Of course we can. Go and wash up first."

Sarah's contagious laughter filled the house and bolstered August's courage. He removed his boots and outer clothing before walking to the rear of the cabin where Katherine bustled about the kitchen.

"Sarah said you're making pie."

"I didn't have the heart to tell her I don't know how. Breads really are the only thing I mastered, but it can't be too difficult. I think I have the turkey figured out." She turned to him then. "I thought to bake it tonight, and then we could take it tomorrow to share with the Collins's, if that's all right with you."

August was in awe of the woman. “It’s perfect.”

She tilted her head in the same way Clara always had when she sensed August wasn’t telling her everything. Instead of waiting for her to ask, he reached out and held her hands gently in his. “Thank you for today, for your understanding. It’s not easy, my work, but it’s important to me. Not more than my daughter of course, and I don’t want you to feel I asked you stay to watch her while I work, but—”

“That’s not why I’m staying, and you never have to wonder if I’ll understand. You have a gift that does not belong to you alone, or to those you love. I can see that this gift is a burden to you at times, but without it, you would not be the man you are. I know why Clara remained with you, even when you felt she desired her old life.”

August wanted nothing more in that second than to kiss her. It wouldn’t be a betrayal to his wife or his daughter, but it would be a welcome beginning to a new journey in his life. He would give them time to know each other, and for her to be sure, but he prayed that she was one Christmas gift who would never go away.

“Are you ready?” Sarah bounced into the room and grinned up at Katherine. “Can we make three pies?”

“Well,” Katherine began, “I have a confession to make.” She smiled and guided Sarah to the kitchen.

August stood by and watched light and joy return to his life.

Katherine was roused from sleep by a dampness on the back of her hand. She tried to brush it away, and then saw Crockett’s big brown eyes staring up at her from the side of the bed. His tail thumped on the rug, and his body twitched and swayed as though he waited for permission to pounce. Katherine stretched and reached over to scratch the dog's ears. Crockett barked once and moved toward the door.

"I'll be along soon." Katherine waited, but the dog seemed content to remain at the door and wait for her to follow. "Very well." She splashed cold water on her face and washed before slipping into one of two dresses that she managed to bring with her on the horse. Odd, but she hadn't thought about the trunk she had left behind in Helena, and made a note to ask August how to get it delivered. Katherine smoothed her loose, raven hair into a knot at the nape of her neck, and with her wool shawl draped over her shoulders, she followed Crockett from the bedroom.

Katherine stopped at the entry to the main living room, giving herself a moment to enjoy the scene before her. August knelt beside the tree, the firelight dancing shadows all around him. Crockett nudged his arm after he set a tall, and impressive, dollhouse next to the tree followed by two wrapped packages placed underneath the hanging boughs. Katherine imagined Sarah spending hours with the beautiful dollhouse and wondered how soon she could get a crate shipped from the East.

"I expected her to be awake by now."

August turned at the sound of her whispered words and grinned. "I only carried her back up to bed an hour ago. I heard her sneak downstairs—another tradition of hers—to look at the tree and wrapped presents before anyone else." He stood and set another log on the fire. "You're up early again."

"It's becoming a habit." Katherine moved to stand beside the fire. "August, there's something I need to tell you."

"Sounds serious." He motioned to one of the chairs in front of the fire. "We have a little time before Sarah wakes to open presents. I know she's anxious to go to town to see Teddy and Ollie."

"Will Ollie truly be all right?"

"I believe so. I'm going to do everything I can to make sure he is."

Katherine admired his long limbs as he settled back into the chair. Her sister had been a lucky woman. "I'm not good at preamble, so I'm just going to say it. Clara left behind a lot of things when she came west, and she never sent for them."

"What kind of things?"

"Childhood possessions mostly, but I believe Clara would want Sarah to have them now. I wanted your permission to send for them."

"Of course, and I'm grateful, but—"

Katherine exhaled and pulled the edges of her shawl close together. "That's only part of it. You see, Clara and I were to split the inheritance that would come from our parents after their death. When Clara passed away before they did, I asked them to keep the will intact. That inheritance is now Sarah's."

August stared at her. Even in the dim light, Katherine saw his eyes remain steady, but she imagined his thoughts were not.

"Clara never said anything."

"She didn't know. When we offered to send her money, she refused. Again, I believed there would be time . . . but it ran out." Katherine reached into her pocket and passed August a folded document. "The details are here. I made the arrangements with our lawyer before I left."

Katherine watched August read the statement declaring Sarah the sole heir to Clara's half of the fortune. She expected some reaction, whether disbelief or anger, she wasn't sure, but she did not expect the quiet.

He looked and refolded the paper. "This is a lot of money."

"It is."

"I know we live modestly, but Sarah doesn't need—"

"I'm not saying either of you need it." Katherine sat forward in the chair, and if she wanted to, she could reach out and touch August, but she kept her hands wrapped in her shawl. "I envy and admire your life, and I don't want you to ever think otherwise. This money isn't about that. It's about Sarah."

August rose from the chair and set the document on the mantel. "I left the East long ago because I saw what wealth was doing to my own family. After my mother died, my father turned to business as a reason for living. My happy memories died with her, and I don't want that for Sarah."

Katherine stepped up beside him and settled her hand on his arm. The heat from even that part of his body warmed her more than the fire. "You're not your family. You and Clara raised a remarkable daughter, and you've done a wonderful job with your life out here. Sarah has a lot of history she's never been told about, and I would like to share it with her."

August lowered his eyes to meet hers. "You want her to have the life that's waiting for you in Boston?"

Katherine slowly shook her head, making the decision in that second, and knowing it was the right one. "I'm selling the houses."

August shifted, but not enough to dislodge her hand from his arm. "What about your father's company?"

"A friend of my father's has made numerous offers to purchase the business over the last several years, and I'm going to accept."

"You came here with this planned?"

Katherine almost laughed. She'd never been one for spontaneity. "I intended to return to my life, the company, society—all of it. I can buy a small house or even a ranch. I don't know what to do with it, but I can live here and be nearby for Sarah. I can't replace my sister, but—"

August stopped the rest of her words with a gentle press of his fingers to her lips. "You're not your sister."

Katherine's excitement deflated faster than her next breath left her body. She tried to move away, but August's hand cupped her face.

"You don't have to be your sister. Be you, Katherine."

August bundled Sarah in a blanket and then covered her and Katherine with a second blanket once they were seated in the wagon. Crockett took his place in the back, alert and excited for another outing. Gift giving had been one of surprise for them all. Sarah squealed with delight when she saw her new dollhouse and unwrapped the two small dolls to go with it. Her delight doubled when Katherine told her that she could have the dolls she and Clara played with as girls.

The most beautiful moment came when Katherine opened her gift. August knew she hadn't expected one, but it made the giving sweeter. He had purchased the locket a few months before, not knowing at the time why except that perhaps Sarah would like the fine piece when she was older. The silver oval on the long chain opened to reveal one picture of Sarah and one of Clara. Katherine's tears had nearly brought on his own. She wore the locket now as the horses carefully navigated the snowy road.

The town was quiet except for a few people either going to see family or headed to the saloon because they didn't have any. Merriment from behind the swinging doors of the saloon brought a smile to August, despite what he knew was taking place inside. The small brown church boasted a ribbon-adorned tree near the front entrance. Wreaths and pine garland graced the doors and balconies of many establishments, including the medical office.

He stopped in front of the clinic and helped Katherine and Sarah down while Crockett bounded from the back and hurried to the door. August carried a heavy basket while Katherine held onto a smaller one. A fire burned in the wood stove, warming the building.

Sarah hurried passed the adults toward the back room, calling out "Merry Christmas!" as she went. August stopped and reached for Katherine's hand. With a light squeeze, he bent down and brushed his lips across her cheek. "Thank you."

Her beautiful blue eyes looked up at him. "Whatever for?"

"A new beginning."

Revelry and cheerful voices blended with Crockett's happy barks. "Pa, Katherine, come see. Ollie's all better!"

Katherine squeezed his hand back. "It's Clara who gave us both a new beginning."

Katherine watched in amazement as the eagle swooped down to the tree and grasped the branches. The great creature settled in and stared off into the distance. If such beauty could be seen from down here, she could only wonder at what glorious sights that eagle saw from its high perch.

She stole these few moments for herself, standing at Clara's snowy grave. Katherine believed her sister would have liked the spot August chose. Nestled in the trees, Clara could still see the cabin, watch her daughter play outside, and her husband work. She could look out over the valley from her place on that mountainside and watch Sarah live a life filled with beautiful memories.

Katherine dared not predict what her future would bring,

but she had found a home on August and Clara's mountain. Christmas carols drifted over the wintry landscape, followed by Sarah's giggles and Crockett's barking. Katherine stood and brushed the snow off her wool skirt.

"I promise that she'll always remember you, Clara."

Katherine glided her fingertips along the top of the stone marker then returned to the warmth of a new found family to celebrate on Christmas Mountain.

The End

Teton Christmas

A Short Story

Wickliffe, Wyoming Territory—December 22, 1892

The sun shone from the brilliant blue sky, kissing her skin and brightening the freckles scattered across her nose. McKensie Stewart closed her eyes, breathed in the frosty air, and spread her arms wide. She stood on the side of the snow-covered road where the stage coach had dropped them off and relished in the wonderment. They had finally arrived in Wyoming.

For years, all McKensie dreamed of was to venture west and write stories about the beauty of the landscape and the interesting people she'd only heard and read about. Submitting articles about society events in Asheville, North Carolina, to the *Weekly Pioneer* hadn't presented much of a challenge. All of that had changed four months ago, and though McKensie wished the circumstances for her final arrival had been more pleasant, she was determined to look ahead instead of mourning what she had left behind.

McKensie spun around in a circle and laughed.

"McKensie! What on earth are you doing?"

She opened her eyes and grinned at her sister. "Is this not magnificent, Maddy? Have you ever seen so much open land or a sky so blue?"

"I can't say that I have." Madison joined her sister's laughter, then settled down and held tightly to her carpetbag. "Aunt Caitlyn should be around here. There she is!"

McKensie clapped her hands in excitement.

"Miss Stewart?"

She glanced up, shielding her eyes from the sun. "Yes."

The man jumped down from the wagon and tipped the edge of his worn hat. "I'm Deke. I work for your aunt, Mrs. Marsh."

"Oh, yes. Aunt Caitlyn has mentioned you in her letters."

She held out her gloved hand, and with some surprise, Deke accepted it.

"It's a wonderful pleasure to meet you, Mr. Deke."

"Just, Deke, miss."

"Then I must insist you call me McKensie."

The older man's gray whiskers and swarthy skin couldn't mask the faint blush on his cheeks. When Deke asked about their luggage, McKensie pointed toward the two trunks and thanked him for looking after them. She turned at the sound of her sister's familiar laughter. Her Aunt Caitlyn walked alongside Madison, her tall willowy frame and flaxen hair a welcome sight and a not-so-subtle reminder of her mother. Her aunt held open her arms, and McKensie rushed toward them, enveloping her aunt in a warm embrace.

"It's been too long, my darling girl." Caitlyn stepped back and looked at them both. "Far too long."

Tears welled, but McKensie was determined not to cry or allow the moment to be filled with sadness. She widened her smile and kissed her aunt's cheek. "Thank you for having us, Aunt Caitlyn."

"You've both grown into beautiful young women. With your stylish good looks and a faint hint of that musical accent, you'll have more suitors than the hotel has rooms."

"I'm not looking for a husband, Aunt Caitlyn. Maddy is the romantic in the family."

Madison swatted her sister's arm, but the action was accompanied by another grin.

"The trunks are loaded, Mrs. Marsh. I'll just take them on over to the hotel."

Caitlyn turned around and watched Deke climb up to the wagon seat. "We'll dine at the hotel before settling in and touring the town. Why don't you join us, Deke?"

"I couldn't be doing that seeing as I'm dust-covered and didn't wear my good hat. I'll just go on over and see Miss Patty at the café." The old man grinned, clucked his tongue a few times, and set the pair of stock horses into a steady walk over the snow.

McKensie smiled at her aunt. "He's delightful."

"And loyal. He's been at the Wickliffe Hotel for more than fifteen years and worked with Phillip's father at the Marsh Ranch before that. I don't know what I would have done without him after Phillip passed." Caitlyn settled one arm around each of her niece's and guided them toward the hotel. "The Wickliffe Hotel serves the best food in the territory, if I do say so myself, and a coffee cake to rival even your mother's."

McKensie and Madison feigned a gasp and Madison said, "I won't believe that until I've tried it." She leaned back and looked at McKensie. "Can you imagine a coffee cake better than mother's?"

"I do believe the fine patrons of the Asheville Lady's

Society would faint from the mere thought that mother's coffee cake could be outdone."

Caitlyn's musical laughter joined her nieces, and she pulled them both closer. "Oh, I have missed you both so much."

McKensie noticed that her aunt looked ready to burst into tears. "Are you all right, Aunt Caitlyn?"

Her aunt nodded and swiped at a few tears on her cheek. "I'm just happy. Come, let's have lunch, and then I'll give you the grand tour of Wickliffe."

McKensie soaked up the holiday atmosphere as they made their way down the road, stopping in front of various storefronts along the way. Despite her aunt's desire to reach the hotel, neither McKensie nor her sister could help but stop and admire the quaint shops—what few there were—and the rustic garland and ribbons decked over windows and doors. She couldn't have expected that the hotel would have gone undecorated for Christmas, but she hoped her aunt left something for them to do.

The Wickliffe Hotel stood at the end of the road, a large wood and brick building with gleaming windows and an expansive porch in front. To McKensie's confusion, the hotel appeared to be the only building in town not decorated with trimmings or even a wreath.

"It's an absolutely lovely hotel, Aunt Caitlyn, but . . ."

"Yes, lovely," Madison added.

"Don't worry, girls." Caitlyn smiled and wrapped one arm around each of them. "We do things up grand here at the Wickliffe, but I thought perhaps you could help me this year."

McKensie turned and stared into her aunt's eyes. The moment had come when she was unable to hold back the tears and a few managed to escape. "Thank you." She leaned in and embraced her aunt, pressing a kiss on her cheek. "Thank you ever so much."

Madison interrupted the precious moment, and McKensie turned to see her sister peeking around the side of the building.

"Wherever did you find one of those out here, Aunt Caitlyn?"

McKensie joined her sister at the edge of the front porch and smiled. Before them waited a shiny horse-drawn sleigh.

"It's not mine, though it does bring a bit of holiday cheer to the place. The sleigh belongs to a guest who will be here over the holiday." Caitlyn hurried the girls inside and out of the cold. "We'll warm up and take our meal while you tell me all about the latest news in Asheville."

Brandon Cutter looked up from his usual table at the Wickliffe Hotel and studied the trio of women who entered the building. The bright winter sun created an ethereal backdrop as they stepped through the glass-paned doors. His own smile grew when he recognized the tall, blond beauty in the center. He then studied the woman's two companions. So these are the Stewart sisters come from the South to experience life on the great frontier.

Neither of them appeared suited to life in the Wyoming mountains, but he supposed if a woman like Caitlyn Marsh could find a way to adapt, then just about anyone could. He smiled, remembering the first day he had met Caitlyn. She'd arrived as a mail-order bride to Phillip Marsh, hotelier and son of a cattle tycoon. Phillip had been about as big and rough of a man to ever walk Wyoming soil. Brandon hadn't been much older than twelve when he started working for Marsh's father at the ranch, and he watched that sweet eastern woman smooth the rough edges of the cattle baron. When the area began to grow, Phillip Marsh built the first and only hotel within 100 miles, and he never looked back. He'd made a fine hotelier before he passed, and his wife had carried on in his stead.

Normally, Brandon would invite her over, but he rather enjoyed watching these women in their reunion. He hadn't seen Caitlyn this bright and shiny since Phillip died from pneumonia two winters ago, and he didn't want to interfere with her joy now. It did give him a chance to give a careful study to her nieces. Both beautiful. They looked so much alike, one might mistake them for twins if they weren't looking closely enough to notice the subtle differences in the shape of their eyes or the fullness of their lips. Caitlyn had described them to him perfectly.

One wore a wool coat the same chestnut color as his favorite Thoroughbred, and moved with an exuberance he rarely saw in young women. She possessed an energy that could not be mistaken or ignored, and Brandon found himself leaning forward to better glimpse her face. Unfortunately, she sat in a chair with her back to him, and his view was now blocked by other patrons.

He finished his meal and thanked the young waitress who had served him at breakfast. Brandon reached for his hat when the niece he had so admired stood, spoke quietly to her aunt, and walked to the lobby area of the hotel.

"Ah, hell." Brandon swore when he saw the two men walk into the hotel lobby, and with hat in hand, walked around the tables attempting to stand between his friend's niece and two men who were better suited to the saloon than the respectable hotel. However, he didn't reach them before they followed the young woman outside.

Brandon stepped out into the cold winter air, only to see

the two cowboys closing in quickly. He watched her spin around and slap away one of the men's hands. Brandon lengthened his stride, stepped around the cowboys, and stood directly behind the young woman, careful not to touch her when he spoke. "I'm a friend of your Aunt Caitlyn's. Whatever I say or do, please just go along with it."

Brilliant green eyes the color of his summer pastures narrowed and then opened wide. If Brandon wasn't mistaken, he'd swear those eyes were flecked with gold dust.

"You ain't out to spoil our fun, now, are you Cutter?"

Brandon turned around, pushing the woman behind him. "You won't find your fun here, boys. The lady is under my protection."

One of the cowboys looked from Brandon to the lady in question, who much to Brandon's irritation, refused to stay out of sight. "You sure about that, Cutter? I done saw her just step off the stagecoach." The cowboy reached out and Brandon gripped his wrist, the action costing him little effort and the other man a good deal of pain. "Fine, Cutter. We're leaving."

Brandon watched them walk away before turning around. He'd planned to scold her, or at the least instruct her on the dangers of walking around town alone when she didn't know who was around or where she was going. Her gold-flecked green eyes stared up at him, and he'd swear she wanted to laugh.

"It's churlish of me to make light of the situation, so instead I will thank you for your chivalry." She peeked around him once and then straightened again. "But wasn't that exciting? I've never met a cowboy before, although I've heard of them and of their behavior. The experience is far better than what one reads in books."

Brandon's head spun and he couldn't decide if she

required a good throttle by her aunt or if he wanted to carry her off into the mountains. Since her aunt was one of his dearest friends, and the only family he had on this earth, he opted for neither.

"Exciting isn't the word for it, Miss Stewart."

McKensie tilted her head back so she could see the man better from beneath her wool bonnet. Tall, with skin touched repeatedly by the sun and hair falling beneath the type of wide-brimmed hat the men out west seemed to favor.

"What would you call it then, if not exciting?"

"Dangerous."

She grinned up at him. "Perhaps, but without a little danger, how can one expect adventure? Besides, I was not so far away from others that I couldn't call out if necessary."

"Your aunt hasn't told you anything about living out here, has she?"

McKensie shrugged. "A great many things, but no, she did not speak of cowboys waiting in the shadows to accost me when I least expect. I may not be from around here, sir, but I promise that I am not a fool with flights of fancy. Dangers lurk in the shadows in Asheville as much as they do here. I simply choose not to dwell on them." She nodded toward the telegraph office. "I had set myself a task, and if you are still worried about my safety, I invite you to join me."

"How do you know I'm not one of those dangerous shadows, Miss Stewart?"

McKensie leaned toward him, grinned, and whispered, "Because, Mr. Cutter, my aunt speaks quite highly of you." She left him to wonder over that and walked into the telegraph office. He didn't follow her inside, but she watched through the window where he stood, waiting by the door like a determined sentinel at his post. When she stepped back outside, McKensie tucked her scarf underneath her chin to ward off the frigid wind that had sneaked up during the brief time she was inside.

"If you don't mind, Mr. Cutter, I do believe I'd prefer the warmth of the hotel right about now."

He smiled and held out his arm, which she gladly accepted as they navigated the icy and snowy road back to the hotel. "You knew who I was the entire time?"

McKensie shook her head. "Not until that wretched man called you Cutter. My aunt described you well in her letters, though I must say I did not expect someone so . . ."

He opened the door to the hotel dining room and waited for her to pass him. "So what?"

"Tall." She didn't bother to hide her amusement. "Won't you join us?" McKensie walked toward the table where her aunt and sister sat, and she noticed with delight that the food had arrived. "Aunt Caitlyn, look who found me outside."

Caitlyn stood and reached for Brandon's hands "I wasn't expecting to see you until tomorrow."

"Unexpected business brought me into town a day early."

"Then we are the ones who shall benefit." Caitlyn indicated the two empty chairs. "Please, join us."

"Thank you, but I must be on my way. I'll return in a few hours for the tree hunt." Brandon smiled as he tipped his hat to the women.

McKensie settled back into her seat. "Tree hunt?"

Caitlyn nodded. "Brandon searches for and cuts down the big tree for this room, and now that you're both here, why don't you two join him and Deke on the hunt?"

Madison scrunched her nose. "In the forest?"

Caitlyn's gay laughter filled the air. "Where else do you suppose we'd find a Christmas tree around here?"

"I'll go."

Two bright pairs of eyes settled on McKensie. She merely shrugged and sipped from the glass of hot cider the waitress set down in front of her. "It will be an adventure, Maddy. Do say you'll come."

Madison shook her head. "You've given me enough adventure for one holiday, and it's only beginning. I'd just as soon decorate on the inside of the hotel."

McKensie spread jam over her warm biscuit and glanced across the table at her sister and then turned her attention to their aunt. "What exactly does one wear when Christmas tree hunting?"

The snow-laden valley stretched out in front of them, backed by the majestic Tetons, a mountain range that far surpassed her expectations of grandeur. The sun peeked through the clouds, casting a halo of light around the high jutted peaks while the wide river snaked through the valley, surrounded by pine trees.

McKensie recalled many of the stories she'd read from journalists who traveled west and then returned east with tales of splendor, wildness, and indescribable beauty. But those writers did not do the land justice nor could any words. The cold barely affected her, so intent she was on the wonder of the breathtaking scenery surrounding her.

She rode a gentle bay mare Deke had secured from the livery and traveled alongside Brandon and Deke to the edge of the forest. When they both dismounted without a thought to where they might land, McKensie realized her predicament. She looked at the ground where Brandon—half a foot taller than her—stood in the snow, but she couldn't see the top of his boots or much of his lower legs, for that matter. She looked down at her own boots, and on a sigh, she mustered her adventurous spirit and dismounted.

Brandon reached her side in seconds, but any effort he might have made to help her down were all for naught. She brushed back her hair, fallen out from beneath the wide hat borrowed from her aunt. Her eyes roamed from the snow, up long legs, and settled on a face lit by amusement.

"Don't you dare laugh."

Brandon's eyes crinkled at the edges when he reached down and deftly lifted her from the two feet of snow she'd landed in. "I wouldn't dream of it."

McKensie brushed away what she could of the snow. "I should have waited for help."

Brandon remained silent.

McKensie huffed and pushed back her hair. "All right, you can laugh." She looked around his broad frame to where Deke stood beside his own horse, ax in hand, his face stoic.

Brandon appeared to be biting the inside of his cheek before he responded with a wide smile. "If you prefer, I can carry you over. The snow isn't quite as deep farther inside the tree line."

"I believe I can manage." McKensie lifted her skirts until they brushed the top of the snow, the action causing her body to shiver. She took one step and then another, mindful that Brandon and Deke both watched. Despite feeling like a sideshow in a carnival, she was pleased with her progress. When she reached the trees, she lowered her skirts and grinned. "That wasn't too difficult."

Brandon watched her brush more snow away, stomp her booted feet once on a bed of snow and pine needles, then walk toward the small trees tucked between the towering pines. He shared a glance with Deke, who barely shrugged and followed McKensie.

A part of him might have wished that she was the type to want a man waiting on her every whim, if only to have had a good reason to carry her. But, he admitted to himself, he admired, and even preferred, her refreshing sense of good humor.

Brandon walked beside her while she examined each tree, remarking on the beauty of one, the brilliant green of another, and the staggering height of yet another. Finally, she stopped and stepped back a few steps from what Brandon assumed was her tree of choice.

"This is the one."

He raised his eyes to the top of the tree nearly five feet above him. "You're sure?"

"It's perfect."

"It's tall," Deke mumbled from behind.

McKensie tilted her head in a way that prompted Brandon to stare at the light spread of freckles over her nose and cheeks and the way her cheeks dimpled when she smiled. When she gently bit the lower lip of her mouth in concentration, Brandon forced himself to turn his attention back to the tree.

"Is it too tall for the hotel?" she asked.

"We'll make it work." If it had been too tall, Brandon still would have found a way to get the tree inside the hotel's lobby where Caitlyn set it up every Christmas. Deke handed him the ax, and Brandon set about the task of cutting the large evergreen while Deke unraveled the rope they would use to haul it back to town.

Once the tree was secured and each end of the rope tied to Deke and Brandon's saddle horns, Brandon stood at the edge of the deep snow, ready to help McKensie back to her horse. Except she wasn't within sight.

"Miss Stewart!" He walked back to where they'd cut down

the tree. He walked half a dozen more yards. "McKensie!"

Deke came up behind him. "How'd that little lady disappear so fast?"

Brandon just shook his head. "Hell if I know. Wait here, Deke, and if she wanders back, tie her to that oversized tree." He headed a short distance past their cutting ground when he noticed the small boot prints in the snow. It wasn't much farther when he saw her bent down, hovering just a foot above the ground. "Miss Stewart."

She spun around on her toes but, bent over as she was, she lost her balance and toppled backward, pinecones tumbling from her arms. Brandon rushed over and quickly pulled her up off the ground.

"Well, that's a fine mess." She brushed away more snow and began to retrieve the fallen pinecones.

"What are you doing?"

"Gathering pinecones."

Brandon's lips twitched even as he hoped she wasn't as addled as she seemed in that moment. "I can see that, but why?"

McKensie finally looked up at him. "To set around." She finished gathering the cones and stood with them in her arms, a smile on her lips and a bit of snow and dirt on her chin.

He wanted to reach out and brush away the bit of snow, but instead he occupied his hands by removing his hat and transferring the cones into it.

"Well, that's kind of you, Mr. Cutter." She looked around him and only must have realized that they were completely alone. "I suppose I did wander off too far. My apologies if I worried you."

Worried him, no, but he had an inkling that she was going to keep them all on their toes. "We don't have a lot of daylight left."

"Will it take long to move—what was that?"

The eerie howl echoed off the nearby mountains followed by a low rumbling blend of growls and screams.

"Those animals aren't close, aren't they?" McKensie dropped the pinecone-filled hat and stepped closer to Brandon, but he had already taken her arm and was guiding her swiftly through the trees.

"Wait!" McKensie pulled away from Brandon and rushed back to where she had dropped his hat. She returned to his side as quickly as she could and handed him the hat.

"Why . . . never mind. Thanks." Brandon once more reached for her hand and held it until they reached Deke and the horses.

Brandon picked her up when they reached the deep snow and carried her to the horse. "Is this really necessary? They sounded so far away." However, the look he gave her said otherwise. He leaned toward her and pointed to the open valley between them and the mountains.

"I don't see them."

"Look to the top of the tree line and then straight across the field."

McKensie focused until she saw movement. "Will they come toward us?"

Brandon shook his head. "The mountain lion is satisfied now and would be more interested in our horses than us, but the wolves are another problem. I'd just as soon get you back to town than wait for them to catch our scent." He checked her stirrups and waited until her reins were securely in hand before mounting his own horse. He pulled a large knife from a sheath at his waist and lifted the rope securing the tree to his saddle.

"What are you doing?"

Brandon glanced up at her. "The tree will slow us down, and we need to get you—"

"I know, get me back to town, but are the wolves really a threat? She looked back to where the small pack had been but saw no sign of them now. "Aunt Caitlyn and Madison will be so disappointed if we come back without a tree."

Brandon glanced over at Deke, who again shrugged as though telling him that she was his problem. Against his better judgment, Brandon sheathed his knife and together, he and Deke set their horses in motion. "Stay beside me."

McKensie kept her eyes wide open and her senses on full alert. She had no idea what she was listening for, or what good it would do her if she knew, but alert she remained. She wasn't about to confess to Brandon how exciting it was to be on the run from wild animals.

Not that they were on the run because not once did the men pick up speed or give her cause to worry. Her aunt warned her that life would be different out here, but isn't that why she came? She and her sister could have remained in Asheville, eventually marrying and starting families of their own, but that wasn't the life McKensie wanted, especially after what she'd lost. She needed to make a life in a place that didn't harbor so many sad memories.

In the months since her parents passed, McKensie was haunted by the painful realization that she would never see them again. Her father wouldn't walk her down the aisle at her wedding, and her mother wouldn't be there to assure her that everything would be all right. So far she was getting exactly what she'd hoped for—an adventure to occupy her thoughts.

The town soon spread out before them, quite small

compared to the vastness of the surrounding forests and valleys, with mountains jutting up from the earth and extending across the land. McKensie glanced over to Brandon, but the question she planned to ask was left unspoken. He watched her, for how long she did not know, but his focus on her remained steady even when her eyes met his.

"Is everything all right, Mr. Cutter?"

"I might ask the same thing, Miss Stewart."

Brandon looked as though he would say more but changed his mind and continued riding in silence. When they stopped in front of the hotel, McKensie noticed Brandon staring once more. Uncertain how she felt about his attention or the studied gaze, she managed to dismount on her own and walk up the steps to the hotel.

"Have you ever seen anything so beautiful?"

"It's tall," said Caitlyn.

"And big," Madison added.

McKensie grinned at her aunt and sister. "Perfect, isn't it?"

"Yes, perfect." Caitlyn looked at the tree and then to Brandon who grinned, and excused himself to help Deke with the horses.

Madison stepped toward her sister, and reached out to pull a twig from her haphazardly coiffed hair. "What exactly happened out there?"

McKensie swatted her sister's hand away. "Christmas tree hunting is not easy business, Maddy, and you would know that if you had come with us." She spun around the large room, noticing the ribbons tied in large bows around the sconces, strings of beads intertwined with greenery hung around the room, and shiny baubles waiting to be set about the tree. "Wherever did you find all of this out here?"

"My dear Phillip indulged my love for the holiday and ordered them from New York years ago."

McKensie pulled off her gloves, careful not to drop pine needles and dirt on the floor. "I think it's marvelous." She calculated the space of the hotel lobby and dining room. "What about a dance?"

"We're not in Asheville any longer."

"I know that, Maddy, but I imagine people in Wyoming know how to dance." McKensie looked over at her aunt. "Don't they?"

Her aunt seemed to consider the idea and then slowly nodded. "I don't know about all the people, but whether they know how or not, I think it's a grand idea." Caitlyn crossed her arms and tapped her chin with a finger, an affectation McKensie realized her aunt shared with her mother. "The town could use a bit of cheering up this season."

Madison sat down in a chair at one of the tables. "What do you mean?"

"It's been a difficult year for some of the families, especially those who have tried to farm. Most people from the cities romanticize life in these mountains, but it takes more than a courageous spirit to survive out here. Had it not been for my Phillip, I would not have remained past the first winter."

McKensie stepped toward her aunt and settled a hand on her arm. "Yet, you did not try to talk us out of coming."

Caitlyn raised a brow, an action McKensie remembered well from her younger years. "My dear girl, if I had tried, would you have stayed away?"

McKensie grinned. "No, and now that we know that, let us get back to the dance. If the townspeople are in need of a little extra holiday cheer, a dance is just the thing to set things to right."

"Dancing doesn't solve the world's problems."

"Nor is it meant to. You used to love dancing, and a bit of extra holiday spirit would be fun." McKensie clapped her hands together and turned around in the open room. "We will host a dance to rival those in Asheville. Elegant women and dapper gentlemen twirling and laughing." She then watched two men, both of whom appeared in need of a good bath, step into the lobby, likely for a meal. One of them had his lips set in a hard line, and the other smiled wide, revealing two straight rows of yellow teeth. McKensie cleared her throat. "Well, somewhat dapper."

Brandon was due back at his ranch, but when Caitlyn invited him to join them for supper in the family's residence located behind the back of the hotel, he couldn't think of a reason not to stay. He could tell himself that he wanted to spend more time with Caitlyn, which was true, or that he preferred a good homemade meal rather than fending for himself at the ranch since his housekeeper recently moved to Montana with her sister's family. What he didn't admit aloud was that he wanted to spend time with McKensie.

She confused him in ways that left him both infuriated and amused. He delighted in her effervescent outlook on life and well, almost everything else. After years of listening to Caitlyn read her sister's letters about the girls, and later the girls' own letters while he and Phillip enjoyed an evening whiskey, Brandon thought he knew McKensie and Madison. Then he met them. Madison had been much as he expected, but her sister had proven to be a surprise wrapped in an enigma, all tied up with a pretty Christmas bow.

Brandon removed his hat and knocked at the front door

of Caitlyn's well-kept cabin. When the door swung open, he seemed to have lost his ability to speak. Sparkling was the only way he could think of to describe McKensie, standing before him in a ruby-red dress trimmed in lace and pearls. It was the kind of elegance he hadn't seen since his last trip to San Francisco and a cultivated beauty he didn't think belonged in the West. Then again, Wycliffe could use a little more sophistication.

McKensie's warm smile and bright eyes offered him the kind of welcome that made a confirmed bachelor change his mind about the future.

"I'm early." The words sounded clumsy to him, but McKensie didn't seem to notice.

"Not at all. Dinner will be set out shortly." She reached for her coat and gloves. "In fact, I was on my way out for a walk."

Brandon moved past her into the house and closed the door. "It's freezing out there, Miss Stewart."

"Please, call me McKensie, and because my sister won't think of it, I give you leave to call her Madison."

"Fine, but it's still freezing out there."

McKensie looked through the narrow window beside the door. "It's not snowing, and the stars look lovely." She shrugged into her coat and pulled on her gloves before reaching for the door handle. "I won't go far, but I want to see the land by moonlight, covered in a blanket of stars." She stepped over the threshold and turned. "Are you coming?"

Brandon glanced toward the hallway where he heard laughter from the kitchen, then stepped outside, closing the door behind him.

"Have you ever seen anything so beautiful?"

Brandon watched her tilt her head back and glance up at

the abundance of stars. The luminous moon cast its beams on the mountain peaks and radiated off the partial icy surface of the Snake River. He knew well enough how glorious the land looked on a bright winter night, but he also realized that sometimes he took that for granted. His eyes lowered from the magnificent sight to settle on McKensie. She'd forgotten a hat, and the moonlight cast a golden hue on her fawn-colored hair.

"I've often dreamed of a sight like this."

"You couldn't see the stars in Asheville?"

"Yes, but they aren't this brilliant." McKensie lowered her head, her eyes meeting his. "I often dreamt of living someplace grand and a bit untamed. My father used to tell us stories of the wild, rugged, and glorious Scottish Highlands where he was born, and I imagined they look a bit like this."

"Your parents never took you?"

McKensie ignored the question and focused on a star shooting across the sky, only to disappear behind the mountains. "When my aunt asked us to come out and live with her, I wanted adventure, that much is true, but I was also running away." McKensie stomped her boots a few times in the snow to help keep her legs warm. "Do you believe it's possible for a person to start over? To leave behind their old life and completely embrace a new one?"

She waited, expecting the perfunctory response she often received.

"No, I don't."

"Why not?"

"Who you were will always be a part of you. It has helped shape you." He looked away from her, and she followed his gaze to see what he found more interesting, but nothing lay in front of them except the forest and mountains. "What was wrong with your old life that you'd want to forget?"

McKensie shuffled her feet and glanced back toward the front door. She expected her aunt or sister to come looking for at her any moment. "I wasn't doing anything of importance or true value with my life. I wrote a lady's column for a weekly paper, I went to parties and dances, and I waited for life to happen."

Brandon surprised her again by closing the distance between them. He gently raised her chin until she could see directly into his eyes.

"You're here. You traveled nearly two thousand miles not knowing what to expect. You didn't scare at the sight of wolves or frighten when you heard a mountain lion attack. Those aren't the actions of someone waiting for something to happen. You're important, and forgetting your past, throwing those memories away, would be to overlook how you became who you are."

He dropped his hand and backed away. McKensie cleared her throat. "And I start with my newfound expertise at Christmas tree hunting."

Brandon blinked once and erupted into laughter. From most women, he might have expected a few tears or perhaps a list of all her shortcomings. However, McKensie was no ordinary woman.

The door swung open and Madison stood just inside, her arms wrapped around her body, likely to ward off the burst of cold. Two sisters, both beautiful and seemingly intelligent, and he suspected that both would find their way in the frontier.

"How can one manage to laugh in this cold?" Madison scanned the area and then looked back at them. "You're both crazy, and it's freezing out here." She motioned them inside with a parting, "Dinner is on the table."

McKensie's gaiety continued as they walked back into the

cabin, and Brandon enjoyed how at ease he felt in her company. The merriment continued throughout the meal, everyone savoring the feast of roast chicken with gravy, sweet potatoes, creamed peas, hot rolls, and a sweet apple cake. Brandon's former housekeeper had done well in the kitchen, but she was rarely imaginative and her meats had always been overcooked. He knew that when he came to Caitlyn's, he'd enjoy a feast. Tonight, the meal was exceptional, as was the company of three remarkable ladies, each trying to find their way in life.

"My compliments to the cook." Brandon nodded toward Caitlyn, but she shook her head.

"I cannot take full credit. It seems my nieces learned a thing or two about running a kitchen."

Since neither sister spoke up, Brandon simply smiled at them both. He caught a glimpse of McKensie's lips twitching, but said nothing.

Once the meal ended and everyone's appetites were sated, Brandon began to say his goodnights.

"You'll join us for breakfast, won't you?" Caitlyn asked.

"I need to check in at the ranch. The men know what they're doing, but I don't like to be away for too long. I'll return before supper."

McKensie walked Brandon to the front door, and he couldn't help but be grateful to Caitlyn for allowing it.

"Thank you for today. I enjoyed tree hunting and the run from the wild animals," McKensie said with a smile.

Brandon noticed her eyes held steady on his, but she didn't blink or move. He'd played enough poker with the stockmen at his ranch to recognize the signs as someone who was hiding something or bluffing, and he doubted she was the bluffing type.

He wanted to peel back each of her layers, but he was fast learning that she was a puzzle still in a dozen pieces. Whether or not she realized it was another matter.

"It was my pleasure, McKensie."

He studied her another moment, and knowing he had to leave soon or risk the other women walking in on something they shouldn't, Brandon nodded once and quietly left the house.

"No!" Sweat dripped down her back and beaded across her forehead, but she didn't feel anything except the ache in her heart. "No, come back!"

"McKensie!"

She felt someone gripping her arms and prayed it was her father. The men must have lied when they told her their parents had died. Why was she in the water? She didn't know how to swim.

"McKensie, sweetheart, wake up."

The soft voice eased through the pounding and screaming, but she wasn't ready to leave. She wasn't ready to say good-bye.

"Please, McKensie. You can do it."

Her sister's gentle pleading finally broke through. McKensie's eyes opened and she then felt the nightgown clinging to her damp body. Her chest rose and fell with each harsh intake of air as she gulped in deep breaths.

She looked up her sister. "It's happening again." The tears flowed freely now as she lifted her knees to her chest and covered her face with her hands. She vaguely heard her aunt and sister talking, and then her aunt left the room. Madison lowered herself onto the edge of the bed, attempting to coax McKensie to look up.

"How long was I—"

"Not long." Madison's eyes lowered briefly.

"What is it?" McKensie wiped the tears away. "What did I say?"

"You talked about swimming."

McKensie's chest constricted and she exhaled. When the nightmares first started, she needn't have worried that her sister would hear everything from down the hall. It wasn't until the first night in the hotel on their journey west that Madison knew about the nightly horrors.

"I don't know what I say, Madison. You can't believe any of it."

"Did you tell me everything that happened?"

Madison hadn't been home when McKensie returned from the docks without their parents, and she sent up a prayer of thanks that her sister had been spared. Should she continue to keep the full truth from her sister? She couldn't answer that now any more than she could the night she told Madison that their parents' hadn't survived the storm.

"We'd best get some sleep." McKensie slipped back down under the covers and turned to face the wall.

The next morning, McKensie's head pounded and the mirror above the washstand reflected bloodshot eyes and unusually pale skin. She splashed cold water on her face until she felt somewhat normal, and then made use of her aunt's washroom. After an indulgent bath, she was ready to face whatever questions her aunt and sister might ask, even going so far as to prepare her responses, because in truth, she didn't want to talk about the nightmares. However, when she saw them in the kitchen a few minutes later, neither said anything about the night before.

McKensie sat down across from her sister, who almost immediately passed her a plate of biscuits. "You have to try one of these. Aunt Caitlyn's recipe is much better than our old cook's."

Caitlyn placed a cup of tea next to McKensie's plate and smiled at her niece. "It's a good thing Mrs. Pran can't hear you, Maddy. I remember how fiercely possessive she was of her kitchen—and her skills."

McKensie reached for a biscuit, her gaze darting between her sister and aunt as they continued to talk about the family's old cook before seguing into a conversation about Madison's former beau. When Madison started to talk about another young man who had asked to court her before they'd left for Wyoming, McKensie wondered how long they'd actually last until someone mentioned the previous night's events.

Thirty minutes later when they'd completed the meal, and Madison had regaled them with stories—most of which McKensie already knew—Caitlyn said she had to be getting to the hotel. Madison promised to join her after she explored the town.

McKensie cleared her dishes from the table and looked around for the water in which to wash it. Finding the kettle still full and warm, she stopped up the sink and poured in a healthy portion of the water and scrubbed her dishes clean. "Yes, Madison, I would love to walk through town with you. Of course, Aunt Caitlyn, I would be happy to help you at the hotel today. It is after all almost Christmas." She flung the drying towel on the counter and looked out the small window above the sink, feeling like a petulant child. Hadn't she told herself that she didn't want to talk about the nightmares? She was in fact grateful that her aunt and sister were considerate of her feelings, so why did their silence on the subject bother her.

McKensie didn't wish to talk about her dreams, at least not with them. She thought the nightmares would go away once she left the city, and during her first two days here, she'd not suffered them once. Did she credit that to the initial excitement? All she wanted was to enjoy this Christmas without the emptiness of her parents' loss darkening her spirit.

McKensie wasn't going to spend these glorious days here wallowing in self-pity. She headed for the front door and bundled her body in warm clothes. She pulled open the front door, and her face collided with a strong fist.

Brandon pulled his hand back immediately and reached for her arms. "I'm so sorry."

McKensie scrunched her nose and rubbed a gloved hand over the bridge of freckles. "No harm done. You barely got me."

Brandon watched for any sign of sadness, but the woman before him seemed as carefree and eager for adventure as when they first met, and her grin proved it. From what Caitlyn had told him not ten minutes ago, one would think that her niece was ready for black shroud. If McKensie was upset, she hid it well.

"You're headed out?"

McKensie nodded and closed the door behind her. "I'd like to see the town, and then I'll help my aunt at the hotel. She glanced up and down the streets. "The town isn't as busy as I imagined it would be for the holidays."

"It won't be this time of year. The hotel will get a few visitors, mostly drifters. Our little town stays quiet in the winter." Brandon fell into step beside her. "Do you mind some company?"

"What happens to your horses when you're here instead of with them?"

Brandon deftly moved her a few feet to the right, sidestepping a passing wagon. "They are in the care of an excellent trainer who prefers the horses' company to mine. I've been back to the ranch to give instructions, but I like to be in town for the holidays." Brandon stopped when she did.

"For my aunt?"

Brandon nodded.

"I'm grateful she's had you since Uncle Phillips's passing. I know mother asked her to come back home, but Aunt Caitlyn refused to leave Wyoming."

McKensie continued to lead the way through town, once in a while stopping in front of a building to look through the window. Wycliffe's population of shops was meager but that didn't prevent her enjoyment in watching the blacksmith tan the leather for a new horse harness or delight with the storekeeper when he set out a basket of wrapped chocolates. McKensie heard they were a delectable treat his wife made each year at Christmas.

Brandon was charmed when she bought a small handful of the chocolates and then passed them out whenever she saw a child. He was captivated when, upon seeing a dog tied up to a post outside the store, she excused herself to purchase a biscuit at the café and then returned to feed it the animal.

It wasn't until they stopped abruptly in front of the town's cemetery that her demeanor changed. Without speaking, McKensie walked slowly to the fence that was half-buried in snow. Only the gate had been freed from the snow and ice, and Brandon saw that more than one set of boots had made tracks to different graves. He waited for her to enter, but she remained on the outside, staring at mounds and tombstones.

"Are your parents alive?"

Brandon stepped up beside her, setting his hands on the top of the gate. "My mother died when I was still a baby—fever took her." He leaned into the fence. "My real father left before I screamed my way into the earth. Phillip was my pa after that."

McKensie turned fully toward him, her mouth agape and her eyes wide. It might not have been his place to reveal just how closely connected he was to Caitlyn, but keeping it from McKensie felt wrong.

"Caitlyn is your step-mother?"

Brandon shrugged. "That's one way to put it. I don't think of her that way, not really, but she is family."

"More than I'd realized." McKensie shook her head and packed through the snow before stopping back in front of the gate. "Why did she not say anything?"

"That's something you'll have to ask her, but I suspect she's trying to keep life here uncomplicated for you and your sister." Brandon nodded toward the cemetery. "I didn't know my real parents, but losing Phillip was like losing a father. Christmas became his favorite time of year because it was Caitlyn's."

McKensie's eyes glimmered, at least that's how they looked to Brandon. He sensed she was fighting a deluge of tears and uncertainty, unlike the vivacious woman he'd met two days ago. Brandon suspected that she didn't do anything half-measure. Her emotions held steady at the surface, whether it was joy, or as he witnessed now, sadness.

"It was my father's favorite time of year, too." McKensie swiped at the falling tears. "He insisted on celebrating the Scottish way, as he called it. He took such pride in the selection of evergreens and holly, and of course . . ." She leaned toward the fence, her words faltering.

Brandon reached for her, hesitantly at first, and then slipped his arms around her waist. The memory of Caitlyn collapsing when she heard of her husband's death rose to the forefront of his thoughts. She hadn't been ready, and even now he saw Caitlyn's sadness when she thought no one was watching.

McKensie pushed away from the fence, reaching for Brandon's arm to steady her, and he willingly remained by her side.

"Thank you." She pulled a plaid handkerchief from a pocket and dabbed around her eyes. "I'm not this person. I don't fall apart at the sight of a cemetery or mention of my parents This time of year . . . the memories."

Brandon slowly released her but remained close. "You don't have to always be strong."

She shrugged. "It's what I do. I'd best head over to the hotel. They'll be wondering where I am."

"Wait." Brandon offered her his arm and felt immense relief when she smiled and accepted. They walked back to the hotel, snow and ice crunching under their boots. A soft snow began to fall. McKensie turned her face up to catch the flakes on her skin.

Brandon was mesmerized by her and not only her beauty. He wanted to help her, to see her bright smile and the vibrant light return to her eyes. No matter how difficult life on the frontier became, Brandon had always believed that nature's majesty could heal any sorrows.

An idea developed and a plan was forged.

Brandon had managed to somehow ease her worries, and by the time they reached the hotel, McKensie felt more like her jovial self.

"There you are!" Madison rushed over and grabbed her sister's arm. McKensie had little choice but to follow her back to the kitchen. Immediately, a delectable scent assailed her senses, and just for a moment, McKensie was back home in Asheville with her mother in the kitchen. The cook stood off to the side, sampling whatever treat Madison was so excited about.

"You must try this." Madison cut a square of the cake and handed it to her sister. She then cut another and handed it to Brandon who stood behind her. McKensie hadn't realized that he'd followed them.

McKensie tried a small corner, and all at once the blend of sweet cake and dried berries tantalized her taste buds. She looked up at her aunt who stood on the other side of the long table, brushing flour from her hands.

"Aunt Caitlyn, this is remarkable."

"Not as good as your mother's."

McKensie shook her head and smiled softly. "It's better, and she would have been proud to admit it."

The cook stepped forward, holding a plate with her half-finished cake. "She's the only one who knows the recipe, your aunt. Won't let me near it." Obviously, the woman didn't mind because she finished off her cake and then set about returning to her duties.

"I'll second that, Caitlyn, but you already know how much I love your coffee cake." Brandon set his empty plate on the table. "Is Deke around?"

Caitlyn pointed over her shoulder. "He's out back at the barn. Our guest with the beautiful sleigh doesn't actually know how to drive it. They collided with a snowbank this morning. Deke's assessing the damage."

"I'll go see about helping him out." Brandon put his hat back on and left through the back door. Curious, McKensie walked to the window and watched as his long legs easily navigated through the snow to the large barn that housed hay and horses for Caitlyn and the hotel.

"You've been enjoying a bit of time with Brandon."

McKensie spun around to find her hand standing just behind her. She hadn't heard her approach. "He's been kind."

"Yes, he is."

Caitlyn was looking at her the same way McKensie's mother used to when attempting to root out one of the girl's secrets. Fortunately, it didn't work now any more than it had when McKensie was a child. Caitlyn leaned closer and lowered her voice to a whisper. "Are you all right? I wasn't going to say anything about last night . . ."

"I wondered why you and Maddy had kept your silence at breakfast."

"We're both worried, of course we are, and I won't mention it again if you tell me not to, but I am here for you."

McKensie reached out and squeezed her aunt's hand. "I'm better now, so there's no cause to worry."

"Look what I've done." Madison lifted an uncooked pie into the air. "It's my first pie. Oh, and the townspeople sing carols on Christmas Eve, McKensie, just like back home. You will join us for the singing, won't you?"

McKensie would find a way to balance her past sorrows with her desire to be undeniably happy in her new life. She couldn't confess to her sister or aunt, but it was almost a daily struggle.

"Of course I will." McKensie squeezed her aunt's hand once more and brightened her smile for Madison's benefit, as much for her own. "But, for now, I'd like to learn the secret to that cake."

The morning soon shifted to the afternoon, and before long, the sun set over the valley. The hotel dining room filled up with locals, stockmen, and even a few drifters looking for a hot meal. A heavy snow filled the sky, blocking McKensie's view of the moonlight touching the mountains and forests.

With her sister and aunt visiting with patrons, McKensie sneaked away for a few quiet minutes alone. The street was empty, and the farther she walked from the hotel, the more the silence set her at ease. Candles burned in windows and snow covered the wreaths and evergreens that hung on doors. A wagon sat unprotected at the edge of town.

McKensie made her way through the deepening snow, scraped off what she could from the wagon, and climbed in the back to sit on the edge. Her long fingers reached for the chain around her neck and rubbed the silver locket.

"We made it. I know it's not what you and Pa wanted for us, but I think you'd be happy to know we're going to be all right."

The snow slowly dissipated enough for McKensie to once again see the mountain peaks, though the forest below remained shrouded in white. Moonlight cut through the clouds creating a pale glow that illuminated the crests.

"I don't know why I was spared, Ma, and I don't know how to tell Maddy. She's happy again. This is a good place for her, even though she pretends she didn't want to come. I wish you were both here."

McKensie felt the slightest movement beneath her and turned to see Brandon standing with one hand on the buckboard. He walked to the back, and without saying a word, wrapped a blanket around her shoulders.

"You shouldn't be out here."

"Am I in danger?"

He grinned. "Not at the moment. I saw you leave the hotel."

McKensie brushed snow off the wagon, clearing the space

next to her. To her pleasure, he joined her. "How long were you standing there?"

"Long enough." Brandon reached over and set his gloved hand on hers. "Want to talk about it? I'm a good listener."

She looked away, back to the mountains. In such a short time, they had become her beacons, symbols of comfort and security. "I was with my parents on the ship. Madison was almost engaged at the time and didn't want to leave Asheville, but I longed to see Scotland. We were only two days at sea when the storm hit, ravaging the ship. I somehow ended up in the water, and I remember my father came in after me. When I woke up again, I was on another ship headed back home. I was told later that my mother and two others had also been swept overboard. They never found my father."

McKensie heard the words as she spoke them. The expected tears did not fall, and the tightness in her chest eased, though she couldn't explain why. She lowered her eyes to see that she was gripping Brandon's hand. "Why was I spared and not them?"

Brandon didn't immediately say anything when she clutched his hand, nor did he move. He finally covered her hand, pressing down gently until she felt some of the pressure ease from her body.

"You're asking the wrong question."

She turned away from the snowy landscape and tilted her head back so she could look into his eyes. Already she felt as though no boundary lay between them, and she could tell him anything. Brandon reminded her a little of her father—strong, brave, and possessing a confidence she'd not been able to achieve.

Brandon seemed completely comfortable with his life, and in contrast, she'd always felt restless as though something was missing. She'd managed to achieve a glimpse of what she tended to call the "unknown," but then it would fade away again until she was left wondering about what might have been.

Here now with Brandon, McKensie once more experienced that surge of hope. The emotional ups and downs of the past year drained her, and it was a sensation she didn't relish. Just when she'd thought it was over and her life had returned to normal, a deluge of sorrow returned.

"I don't understand what you mean, Brandon. What other question is there?"

Carolers began to sing, and their songs of merriment drifted from the hotel. McKensie closed her eyes against the onslaught of tears. She wanted to be in that hotel, singing and dancing and remembering everything beautiful about her parents. Brandon gently pulled her toward him, and she eased into his embrace. Her shoulders relaxed and her head lay against his chest as his calm voice of reason soothed her.

"How do you honor them? By living your life and remembering that they lived theirs."

She leaned back enough to look at him. "They had so much more to do."

"We always have more to do. When I was a child, and missing parents I didn't know, Phillip told me to never count on tomorrow because we may have only today. My parents were strangers to me, and yet I still mourned them. We honor those who have gone by living and perhaps by doing those things they didn't get a chance to do."

McKensie smiled, even as tears fell in streams down her face. "They did love adventures. My sister teases that I inherited all of their passion for travel and exploration and left nothing for her."

Brandon removed one of his gloves and smoothed away

her tears. "What else did they love?"

"Family. I was a lucky one because our home was filled with love. I believe that's why my father enjoyed this time of year so much, for what it represented to him."

"Jingle Bells" floated through the air. McKensie laughed, swearing she could recognize her sister's exuberant voice mingling with the other carolers. "That was my mother's favorite song."

"There will be a time soon when the memory of them will be a comfort, and you'll remember them with joy when you tell your children and grandchildren all about your intrepid parents."

Brandon scooted off the back of the wagon and lifted McKensie down, the blanket still draped over her shoulders. The snow had cleared completely, revealing vibrant stars on a backdrop of deepest, darkest blue.

"I'm surprised they haven't come looking for me."

Brandon folded her arm with his. "I might have mentioned something to Caitlyn before I followed you."

"She trusts you."

"As I do her."

McKensie walked close to him, her long legs almost keeping up with his as they ventured back through the snow to the hotel. "My father used to take us all to the mountains to enjoy the first snowfall of the season, and there was something else he loved doing."

"What was that?"

McKensie unhooked her arm from Brandon's, dropped the blanket, and stepped a few feet away. With her back to him, she reached down and gathered snow into her hands.

"What are you doing, McKensie?"

She turned around, and let the snowball soar through the

air, hitting Brandon in the center of his broad chest. The giggle escaped on its own, but it was the most wonderful feeling. "It's a time-honored tradition in my family." She reached down to form another ball, but soon realized that Brandon was not her average opponent when a soft spray of snow covered her face. McKensie hurried to fling another ball at Brandon, only she no longer felt the ground beneath her feet.

Deep laughter filled the air, mingling with hers, and strong arms spun her around until the earth seemed to spin around her. Brandon set her back down and held her close. He brushed her fallen locks of hair out of her face. The singers finished the final verse of "O Christmas Tree" and now the world around them was once again silent.

"Never count on tomorrow because we may have only today." McKensie knew exactly what she wanted for today and all of her tomorrows. "Do you believe that still?"

"I do."

"But it doesn't hurt to plan for tomorrow."

Brandon shook his head. "Will your tomorrows be here or someplace else?"

McKensie knew there would still be days when her heart would ache for her parents, but in this moment, the demons had been chased away.

"I want to see Scotland, just as my father wished me to see it. There are so many places I long to see, and I will see them, but I'm home now. It's not the home I might have once imagined, but it's the one I've chosen." She looked around at the darkness around her. "I don't know what my tomorrows will bring."

Brandon brought her close to his strong body. "I'd like to be there when you find out—no matter how long it takes."

McKensie gripped his arms. "I'd like that, more than I can

say." Despite the warmth from his body, hers began to shiver. "But right now, I don't think I can feel my toes." Her words were spoken on a laugh, and then strong arms lifted her against a warm chest.

"I'll put you down before anyone sees."

She might have been indignant given the improper handling of her person, but since Brandon was warm, she wasn't going to argue. Instead, she huddled into his body and closed her eyes. The world might close in around her, and it may take her a while yet to accept what had happened when she lost her parents to the sea, but today, peace and hope filled her soul.

McKensie opened one eye and then the other, stretching beneath the warm covers. Her lips spread into a smile when she inhaled. The fragrant aroma of something delectable drew her fully awake. She bundled into her robe and walked on stockinged feet to the kitchen. Her aunt wasn't anywhere to be seen or heard. McKensie padded across the floor to the table and lifted a piece of paper that lay beside two plates, each with a slice of coffee cake.

Don't dawdle. Enjoy your cake and then hurry over to the hotel. The day is only beginning, and someone has a surprise for you both.

Merry Christmas, my darling girls.

"Maddy, will you please hurry?" McKensie stood in the open doorway, pounding her boots against the ground and rubbing her arms for warmth.

"Christmas celebrations aren't going to start without us." Madison wrapped her scarf around her neck and joined her sister outside.

"I know that." McKensie clasped her sister's hand and walked on a path that Brandon cleared away after the fresh snowfall. "Did you not read the note carefully? There's a surprise. I do love surprises."

"And it will still be a surprise when—" Madison fell against McKensie's back, nearly toppling them both. "What are you doing?"

McKensie raised her hand and pointed. Before them stood two of the most beautiful white-and-black patched horses she'd ever seen. The harnesses and red sleigh were draped in evergreens and ribbons. A sprig of holly was attached to the bridle of each horse.

Both in awe, McKensie and Madison walked toward the sleigh, McKensie veering off to approach the beautiful creatures. She removed a glove and brushed her hand along the neck of the horse closest to her, its hair smooth and warm beneath her bare fingers. Brandon walked up beside her, holding a small wool blanket, which he draped over her shoulders.

"They're magnificent."

Brandon set his hand on the horse's back. "They're two of my greatest joys, and they love attention." As though sensing they were being spoken of, the animals whinnied.

"You did all of this for us?"

He leaned closer, his warm breath touching her skin. "I did. We may not be able to count on tomorrow, but that doesn't stop us from hoping and dreaming. Today is Christmas, filled with memories past—good memories. It's the first Christmas you'll spend without your parents, but you have family here. I want to see you smile today and every day to come."

McKensie linked her arm with Brandon's, her smile bright and her heart at peace. "How long do we get to use the sleigh?"

"Until the snow thaws in the spring." Brandon grinned. "I bought it. The previous owner decided trains and hired coaches were preferable to driving into snowbanks."

They stopped beside the open sleigh, and McKensie called out to her sister. "Are you coming?"

"I wouldn't miss it!"

Brandon left the sisters by the wagon and walked to the porch where Caitlyn stood on the top step. "We're not going without you."

McKensie saw a slight blush in her aunt's cheeks, and her own eyes filled with moisture. Brandon helped Caitlyn and Madison into the back of the sleigh, and then assisted McKensie into the front. Once they'd all settled under the blankets, Brandon joined McKensie in the front and picked up the reins.

"Merry Christmas, McKensie."

"Merry Christmas, Brandon."

With an exuberant nod of their heads, the horses pulled the sleigh away from the hotel. McKensie huddled under the blanket, and her sister struck up the beginnings of "Jingle Bells."

The End

The recipe for the
Wycliffe Hotel's Famous Coffee Cake
can be found at the end of the book.

Lily's Christmas Wish

A Short Story

Cotter's Gulch, Colorado—December 1868

Dear God. Please help me find a family. Love, Lily.

The forged wheels whirred and ground against the iron rails as the small window of the train car opened up to the vast landscape of the American West. Miss Abbott told her the same stories over and over again, promising that a new life waited. She wasn't sorry to see the dingy city disappear four days ago, and she hoped to never see it again. Those memories she wanted to leave far behind.

Lily believed in her younger years that Miss Abbott had already taught her everything about life, but the teacher promised it would take more than book learning to withstand the laborious life in the West. Lily sat alone on her bench, her eyes absorbing the unfamiliar setting beyond the wooden car. She didn't need to look to know that the person who sat down beside her was Miss Abbott. The teacher always smelled like roses. Two bushes of red roses grew in the small, unkempt garden of the orphanage. Despite years of neglect, the roses found a way to survive—like Lily.

"We're almost there."

Lily slowly nodded and continued to watch as the

mountains moved closer and closer. The temperature dropped. Lily shivered and closed the small window. “Are you scared, Miss Abbott?”

“Not even a little scared. This is going to be a better life for everyone.”

“Will you be adopted, too?”

Miss Abbott smiled, and Lily realized her question was a foolish one. They don’t adopt grown-ups. The teacher didn’t have to come west, but she wanted to be with the children. Lily heard Miss Abbott say so to Mr. Francis at the orphanage. Mr. Francis told her that if the teacher left, she couldn’t go back, but Lily didn’t think Miss Abbott would mind staying in the West. She seemed to like adventures.

“They don’t adopt someone my age, Lily, but I’ll find a nice school and teach children, as I’ve taught you.”

“Will you still be my teacher?”

Miss Abbott smoothed back a curl and tucked it back under her bonnet. Lily thought Miss Abbott had the prettiest yellow hair she’d ever seen.

“I don’t know, but I hope so.”

Lily leaned into her teacher’s arms and turned back to the window. Almost home!

Rebecca Abbott watched in silence as one building became two and soon became the town of Cotter’s Gulch. She wrapped her arm around Lily’s small shoulders and calmed her breathing. She wasn’t scared, but nervousness caused her mind to worry over the children under her charge. She was one of three who escorted the orphans west, but unlike the other two adults, she wasn’t going back.

She promised to always tell Lily the truth, but how did one tell a ten-year-old girl that she may never see her again? Rebecca had offered to adopt Lily, but the orphanage administrators had deemed her too young and unable to support a child on her own. Rebecca knew that Lily’s chances may be better with a family who already had a home, but she'd heard how unpredictable life could be in the West. She vowed Lily would go to a good home or no home at all.

The train whistled, and the wheels rolled to a stop. Passengers began to disembark from the cars, all except for the children in the orphan car. They waited quietly, their interest, excitement, and trepidation mingling together.

"Will we get new families today?"

Rebecca peered into Lily's wide blue eyes, unable to find the reassuring words Lily needed, without lying.

"I'm not certain. It could be a few days."

Lily's sweet disposition and quick mind would make any family proud to call her their own, but Rebecca knew it would take more than Lily's smile and love of learning to win a place in a stranger's home.

Rebecca stood when the head escort called out instructions to the children. Moments later, they filed out of the train car, paired and holding hands. Rebecca stood at the back of the car waiting for each child to step outside. Lily held her hand tightly. Rebecca continued to smile, but how long could she contain her own uncertainty? They stepped down onto the train platform, and Rebecca saw the American West for the first time without the dinge and dust of a square window blocking her view. Unobstructed, the far-reaching blue sky, not a cloud marring its expanse and the imposing peaks, aided to alleviate her jitters.

"Miss Abbott?"

Rebecca turned and ignored the disapproving glare of Miss Cranmore, the supervisor for their little adventure and sister-in-law to Mr. Francis. Miss Cranmore had traveled to the West twice before, each time knowing she could return to the comforts and security of home and a position at the New York orphanage. Seeing now what she only once dreamed, Rebecca could not imagine returning to the din of city life and vowed, with confidence or rather with resolve, to make a good home for herself and to find a good family for Lily.

They joined the line and listened intently to Miss Cranmore's somewhat unfriendly instructions, but Rebecca would not let the older woman's disapproval deter her own wonder and hope for the future.

The train rolled out of the station. This was the end of the line for the orphans, and Rebecca's last link to the past.

Liam Cassidy read the poster announcing the arrival of the orphans. He passed the same poster in three different storefront windows. WANTED: HOMES FOR CHILDREN. He scanned the rest of the poster and shook his head. Ten children put on display like cattle at an auction. Liam continued walking, heard the train whistle as the engine pulled away from the depot, and changed direction.

The children all appeared to be between eight and twelve and stood in a long row at the back of the church. Liam kept to the sidelines and studied the children as one by one they were picked out by an old man, a young couple, or a family with already too many mouths to feed. The entire process sickened Liam, even as he acknowledged that perhaps some of the children might be better off with the good people of Cotter's Gulch.

A young girl, perhaps nine or ten, eyes bright and smile grim, appeared to inspect each person in the room, as though it was she and not them on display for her choosing. Liam waited for her gaze to settle on him, an easy feat since he stood nearly a head taller than most in the room. Blue eyes, bluer than the sky. Hair, long and golden, shone like the sun on a summer day.

Even in the cold of winter, the girl did not shiver or huddle within herself. She kept shifting her gaze to someone on the opposite side of the crowd, but after another survey of the room, she looked at him once more. Liam choked back a rising pain of a memory from his own youth. The girl continued to stare at him, almost defiantly, and yet he believed what he truly witnessed was a determined child grasping onto hope. He almost stepped forward and spoke out, but hesitated. Liam swore he saw disappointment in the girl's eyes.

Two more children remained, and it was now the girl's turn to step forward. It took only seconds before the first voice spoke up. Even if Liam could not see the man in the crowd, he would know the voice. The townspeople huddled together in part because of a lack of space, and in part for warmth, so it took a minute for Amos Ward to step to the front of the group. Liam held himself back from driving Amos right back out of the church, and he'd be willing to bet his ranch that others in the room were of the same mind.

"I'll take her." Liam almost didn't believe the unwavering words were his own. He moved away from the wall, drawing everyone's eyes to him. The girl's eyes darted back and forth between him and Amos. The hope he once saw had been squashed by fear. Liam put himself between the girl and Amos.

"You got no right, Cassidy. I called out first."

Liam hated forcing a scene, but he knew Amos wouldn't back down without one. He also knew the requirements for taking on a child had to be met to the Children's Society's satisfaction.

"Walk away, Amos." Liam whispered in an effort to keep the girl from hearing. He didn't care what the rest of the town heard, or what they thought.

"I won't. I came here for an orphan, and I am to leave with one." Amos stood as tall as he could and managed to reach as high as Liam's chin.

"Let's leave it to them to decide."

Amos looked over at the three administrators who had moved forward, one man, two women. He appeared to be considering Liam's suggestion, and just when Liam was certain Amos was going to cause a ruckus, the reverend stepped forward and spoke quietly. Amos grumbled, his dark eyes boring into Liam, but he quieted and nodded once.

Liam silently thanked the reverend with his own nod. Now everyone was more intent on what would happen next between Liam, Amos, and the young girl. The room's occupants remained silent. Liam ignored them and turned his attention to the administrators, and for the first time noticed the youngest among them. Fair skin, a pert nose, full lips set in a straight line, and eyes, gray and fierce, with a hint of warning. The woman's focus and concern was without a doubt on the young girl, but her distrust fixated on Liam and Amos.

Rebecca's heart thudded wildly within her chest. Every instinct wailed within her to shout and deny both men claims to Lily. They could not have her, but what could she do? The Society would not allow Rebecca to keep Lily unless they were unable to find a family, and now Rebecca's fears crashed into her reality. What a foolish hope to keep Lily with her. To be her mother, her friend, and her protector. What did she know of being a mother? A true mother would find a way to protect this beautiful child from anyone.

Rebecca continued to glare at both men, but it was the taller one who kept her attention. Her initial fear slowly ebbed as she studied him carefully. He didn't shirk away from her scrutiny. His features, though hard, did not appear unkind. He had spoken up when the gray-haired man first made a claim, and there was no mistaking the man's true nature.

"You sure you want a girl, Cassidy? How about one of them strong boys to work your ranch?"

Rebecca didn't see who had spoken, but the man he called Cassidy ignored everything except for her and Lily. He was waiting for them to make a decision.

"Miss Abbott."

Rebecca moved to the back of the church with Miss Cranmore and Mr. Beadle. Their heady discussion did not last long. Mr. Beadle turned to the room as the official spokesman for the Children's Society. "We will move on and then speak with the two gentlemen alone."

The remaining boy was quickly welcomed into a new family, leaving Lily standing alone at the front of the church. Rebecca ushered Lily to her side as the crowd dispersed, except for the gray-haired man and the one called Cassidy.

Mr. Beadle stepped forward, his narrow eyes seeming to study each man as though he could determine their merits within seconds. Rebecca didn't care if she had to defy Mr. Beadle and run away, towing Lily with her. She could not, would not, allow the steely-eyed man to take Lily.

Mr. Beadle finally spoke, his voice calm, brooking no argument. Rebecca had always disliked the sound of his voice. "Mr. Cassidy, is it?"

The man nodded, and to a quick glance, one might think he was bored, but Rebecca had been studying him long enough to notice the tick in his cheek and the hard set of his jaw. He kept his stance relaxed, but his fingers were closed up as though in a fist.

"Did you come here today intent on finding a child? You did not speak out until Mr. . . ." Mr. Beadle turned to the other man. "I'm sorry, sir. Your name?"

"Amos Ward, and I spoke up first."

"Yes, well, Mr. Ward, it doesn't always work that way. We are tasked with ensuring that each child goes to the best home we can find." Mr. Beadle looked back to Cassidy. "Now, Mr. Cassidy. Did you come here looking for a child?"

"No, sir."

Rebecca felt her chest constrict, though why she couldn't say. Fear that Mr. Cassidy would change his mind about wanting a child, or that he wouldn't? She saw him glance once more at Mr. Ward.

"I may not have come here with that intent, Mr. Beadle, but I am decided."

Rebecca listened as Mr. Beadle asked each man the

same questions asked of everyone who took home a child today. Not one question addressed a person's ability to love and cherish a child. She knew her ideas were fanciful. Better a roof over their head and food in their bellies than a life on city streets or in an overcrowded and overburdened orphanage, but did no one think of loving these children? Wanting them for more than servants or ranch hands?

Rebecca half-listened, doing her best to comfort Lily, who for the first time since they left New York, shook with fear.

"I have no intention of working the girl on my land."

Rebecca caught Mr. Cassidy's last sentence and raised her head. He must have already been looking her way because their eyes met.

"What are your intentions?"

Mr. Cassidy's annoyance showed. He seemed as exhausted of this conversation as Rebecca was.

"Ranching is hard enough for a grown man. Besides, I have no need for extra help. She'll go to school, a few chores because every child should have them, but beyond that, she can just be a kid."

"Now that ain't right," Mr. Ward interjected. "Jest because Cassidy here doesn't need help, doesn't give him the right to have her when I spoke first."

Mr. Beadle turned to Mr. Ward. "No, it does not. However, and I don't say this often, Mr. Ward, I don't like you, and I don't believe your intentions toward the girl are honorable."

Rebecca turned Lily's head away in case an altercation took place, and Miss Cranmore put her considerable girth in front of them, blocking Lily's view.

"You won't get away with this, Cassidy."

"I already have, Amos. Don't let me see you at another one of these."

To Rebecca, it appeared that Mr. Ward wasn't going to go quietly, but he eventually turned and left, though not without sending a few more threats Cassidy's way. She soothed Lily into staying with Miss Cranmore and walked to Mr. Beadle, asking him for a private conversation.

"I'm not certain why you did it, but I want to thank you for what you've done for Lily."

Mr. Beadle looked around at the young girl. "It's no secret that I don't always have a way with children, but every once in a while a child comes into our care who inspires hope for what we're doing. Our young Lily Donnelly is one of those children." He narrowed his eyes, and for the briefest moment, Rebecca thought he might smile. "Besides, if I did not ensure she went to a good home, I would have to fetch the sheriff, for surely you would have run away with her."

Rebecca felt the heat creep into her face. "Yes, sir."

"I don't need to ask if you're all right with the decision, but I believe Mr. Cassidy will be good to the child."

"You won't let me keep her?"

"I believe you would be a good mother to Lily, but you know I cannot. You have no home yet, Miss Abbott, and no employment."

"I understand."

"Do you?"

She nodded. "May I speak with Mr. Cassidy first?"

Mr. Beadle considered her request and nodded once before walking back to Miss Cranmore and Lily. A deep, restorative breath filled Rebecca's lungs before she closed the distance between the man who would assume responsibility and care of her beautiful Lily.

"Mr. Cassidy?"

He nodded. "Miss Abbott."

"How—"

"Mr. Beadle informed me of your concerns. If you'll indulge me for a few minutes, I may be able to waylay some of those fears."

"I don't see how, but I appreciate your effort to try."

He smiled a beautiful and warm smile, and Rebecca

almost forgot he was about to take Lily from her.

"I have a ranch not too far from town. I don't know what you intend to do for employment, but I'd be happy to take you on. You can be the girl's teacher and companion."

"I don't understand." And Rebecca didn't. She was willing to fight to get Lily back, and here she was presented with a chance to never leave her. Could she trust him? It didn't matter. She would be with Lily.

"Truth is, I'm not used to children, and I certainly don't know what to do for a young girl. It's a simple life, but I can promise you'd both be looked after."

Rebecca eagerly accepted. "Is this all because of Mr. Ward?"

Mr. Cassidy's eyes darkened, his body stiffened. Rebecca didn't know what she had said to upset him, but he answered her, despite his now shadowed mood.

"He'll have taken insult to what I did today. Just be sure not to find yourself alone when you leave the ranch."

"You'll really take us both with you?"

He nodded. "It seems we can help each other. Besides, Christmas is in a few days, and I don't think it's right to take the girl away from you. Appears you're the closest thing to a family she has, and I'd wager she's rather attached to you."

Rebecca looked across the room at Lily who stood apart from Miss Cranmore and Mr. Beadle, almost defiant in her refusal to be with them. All she wanted was for Lily to be with a family who could love and care for her. Mr. Cassidy's proposal was not ideal, but it would keep them together at least a short while longer. Rebecca promised Lily that she would have a real Christmas, and it was one promise she was now able to keep.

She faced Mr. Cassidy once more, leaning back to look up into his warm, brown eyes. "All right, Mr. Cassidy. We'll both go with you."

Liam walked out of the general store with two wool blankets

and a fur hat, items he hadn't intended to buy, but somehow found pleasure in knowing they were for someone else. He could claim that some unknown force drove him to the church, speak out against Amos Ward, and agree to take home a young girl and her protector. He could claim that, but it wouldn't be true. Liam thought the memories had finally left him alone, but when he saw those children, it was as though the last twenty-three years had slipped away.

He climbed up to the seat of the wagon he rented from the blacksmith and tied his horse to the back. Liam handed a blanket to each of the women. He avoided looking too long at Miss Abbott, as he wasn't entirely certain what prompted the invite to her from his lips. Taking on a child was one thing, but a woman who looks like Miss Abbott, alone in his house with nothing but an aging housekeeper may not be the wisest decision he'd ever made.

Liam did it for Lily.

If he'd continue to remind himself of that, they'd get along just fine. Liam helped tuck one of the blankets under Lily's legs, then paused when he caught her staring, quite unabashedly. She watched him from beneath the fur hat he'd bought, saying nothing.

"The ranch isn't too far from here."

"Thank you, Mr. Cassidy."

Liam enjoyed the comfortable manner in which Miss Abbott wrapped her arm around Lily's shoulders. If he hadn't known differently, and if Miss Abbott had been a few years older, he might have believed they were mother and daughter.

"Call me Liam."

Lily gaped, entranced by the ranch that spread out before her. Mr. Cassidy thought she hadn't been listening when he described his home, explaining to them where they'd sleep and how many other people lived in the house. She had been listening, but his explanations hadn't done it justice. He said it was a modest house. Lily knew what that meant because Miss Abbott had taught her well, but Mr. Cassidy was wrong.

It was the prettiest house she'd ever seen, which meant it was probably too good to be true.

She kept her silence as the grown-ups talked. Lily would guess that Mr. Cassidy wasn't someone who liked to talk much, but he appeared to like to talk with Miss Abbott. Lily didn't even say anything when she walked past them to stare out at the snowy pastures and cattle. She'd seen the animals from a distance through the train window, but somehow they seemed much bigger when a dirty train window wasn't in the way. They smelled, but not too bad. The streets around the orphanage smelled rotten like when the kitchen workers forgot to take out the trash, but here everything smelled fresh without anything to ruin it.

Lily turned her face into the sudden cold wind. The snowflakes began to hit her face one by one until a rush of them nearly knocked her over.

"Lily!"

She heard Miss Abbott, but it's wasn't her teacher's arms that scooped her up and ran toward the house. Mr. Cassidy set her feet down on the front porch and smiled down at her, showing her his nice white teeth.

"Weather can change fast around here."

Miss Abbott knelt in front of her and smoothed away some of the snow from Lily's hair. "How did you wander off so far without me noticing?"

Lily grinned. She knew why Miss Abbott didn't notice, but she didn't say so. She decided to like Mr. Cassidy. Lily liked people, but she didn't trust many of them. Miss Abbott told her to be careful of whom she trusted, but she wanted to trust the stranger who brought them home and had a nice smile. He also stopped the other man from taking her home, and for that reason, she would not only trust Mr. Cassidy, but she would like him, too.

"I wanted to see the animals."

Mr. Cassidy shuffled Lily into the house with Miss Abbott.

"I'll give you a tour of the property when the storm lets up. It shouldn't last too long, but you never know around here. I'll introduce you to Mrs. Cooney. She's the housekeeper and cook, and then we'll get you settled in."

Lily and Miss Abbott followed Liam down the short hallway to the kitchen where a robust, gray-haired woman sang while pulling something from the oven.

"We have guests, Mrs. Cooney."

The woman turned and settled her hands on her hips. "So we do, but you don't leave them standing in the doorway. Come on in here and warm yourselves by the fire, and don't mind him. Call me Ida."

Liam exhaled the breath he felt he'd been holding since he agreed to bring the woman and child home with him. At least now they'd be in good hands with Mrs. Cooney. He, on the other hand, had some explaining to do. Ida filled tea cups and set a plate of scones on the table, then pointed to the hallway where Liam obediently went.

"Where'd you get two lovely young ladies like these, Liam Cassidy?"

Ida's thick Irish brogue scolded as much as it did when he, as a young boy, first came to Colorado. Liam explained what happened in town. He knew Ida would understand seeing as how she was there when he and Alec stepped off the train with no idea what the future held for them.

"You did what you had to, then, and I'm proud of you for it." She wiped her hands on her apron and indicated the pair who Liam now watched over Ida's shoulder. "I know good people when I see them, but I know hurt ones, too. What do you plan for them?"

Liam hadn't thought beyond the now. They'd stay for Christmas, but what about the after? Would they want to remain here or move on? He committed to caring for the girl and he promised Miss Abbott a job—he aimed to keep both promises—but he couldn't force them to stay. The slip of paper Mr. Beadle had given him may give him the right and responsibility of Lily, but he believed the decision to stay would be up to them. Did he want them to remain here at the ranch? To live with him and Ida until Lily was old enough to make her own choices and live her own life? He'd have time later to ponder his thoughts further.

"I don't know what's going to happen, but no one comes in on those orphan trains who doesn't need a home. I mean to give them a home for as long as they want one."

Ida nodded as though she could see what came next for all of them. "The men came asking for you earlier—something about cows and the north fence. I'll get those young ladies settled in, don't you go worrying about them."

"Thank you. I am grateful. I know I've sprung this on you—"

"You never mind that. It will be nice to have some female companionship around here."

"I don't deserve you." Liam kissed her cheek and swiped a biscuit from the basket on the counter.

"No, you don't. Now get." Ida swatted him away, but her grin told Liam that his affection for her was reciprocated.

Liam dealt with questions from his foreman and got to work, helping some of the men with fallen fence lines and gathering strays. He rarely left all of the grunt work to the ranch hands, preferring to sweat and toil as much as the next man. He came to Colorado with nothing but fear and a few dreams, working from sunup to sundown until his back ached and his hands hurt from the scrapes and cuts of hard labor.

For more than twenty years, he worked Roane's ranch, starting at the bottom as a young man and working his way up to foreman of the ranch he currently owned. Most of the folks hadn't treated orphans well back then, but Roane

Cassidy gave him a chance. Beaten and half-starved, Liam hadn't been willing to trust anyone, but Roane had earned his trust, put him to work, and became his family. When Roane passed on five winters ago, Liam was grateful for Ida's presence in his home, and for the loyal men who stayed on at the ranch. Liam earned their respect, and the men didn't begrudge the young orphan, who had become a strong and capable man, his right to the land.

Liam hadn't given much thought to what would happen to the ranch after he passed on—which in this life could be at any time—but he supposed being the legal guardian now of Lily, the ranch would pass to her. Liam stopped, the wire temporarily going limp in his hands. He liked the idea of her getting the same chance Roane had given him, but what did Lily know of ranching?

"Well, hell."

"You say something, boss?"

"No." Liam stretched the wire and finished securing it to the post. He handed the tools to the worker who toiled beside him. "I'm going to ride the fence through those trees, and I'll see you back at the ranch."

"I can do that for you."

Liam shook his head. "Thanks, but I could use the ride." Liam mounted his strong and sure-footed Appaloosa, and headed for the trees through the snow. He did need the ride, but what he needed more was time to consider how his new relationship with Lily and Miss Abbott was going to work. The Smokey Creek Ranch had been his first real home, and as fate would have it, the first place he'd ever known what Christmas was like with people who cared about him. He wanted that for Lily, if for no other reason than to do for someone what Roane Cassidy had done for him.

He didn't expect Lily to take his name as he'd done Roane's, but he would carry out the promise he'd made to her and to Roane. He'd promised the old man that he wouldn't live his life alone. Liam had been too busy and had forgotten that promise over the years, but the plain fact was, now he had a reason to remember.

The remaining fences were in good enough repair to see them through the coming winter storms. They'd been lucky so far without too much snow on the ground to hinder the stock, but Liam always could feel when Mother Nature was about to wreak havoc on them. The trees to the north would block much of the snow that usually blew down the mountain toward the cabin. A Christmas tree. He didn't have one up at the house, and Christmas was only a few days away. He normally cut one down the day before Christmas Eve, generally being too busy to get one up sooner, but this year should be different for Lily.

Liam pushed his Appaloosa into a gentle canter, enjoying the light spray of snow the horse's hooves kicked up as they made their way across the open fields. The cold mountain air invigorated him, the snow subsided, and the sun beat down upon them. Liam rode through the cattle to the corrals and on to the house, passing men who hurried to get their work done before night descended.

Liam dismounted at the barn, took care of settling his horse in for the night, and headed up to the house. Halfway there, he stopped a moment to look at the structure. Built to withstand the elements and time, Smokey Creek Ranch had survived more winters than years Liam had been on the earth. The place had needed little more than a few roof repairs after some harsh winters and storms, and some boards replaced here and there on the big porch. He had promised Roane that he'd look after the place. It would be a shame not to have it pass on to someone who might love the place as much he did.

Liam was barely three steps from the front door when it opened. Lily stood just under the threshold, her worn, but clean wool coat, buttoned up to her neck. A thick scarf was wrapped around her neck.

"Ida said it might snow again and said not to call her

Mrs. Cooney because it made her feel old." Lily tilted her head, and her bright eyes narrowed up at the sky behind him. "It doesn't look like snow is coming."

Liam chuckled and motioned her to step outside. "Ida'll have both our heads if we let all the heat out of the house. Come on over here." Liam stepped to the railing and waited for Lily to join him. "We get a lot of sun out here, but see there over the mountains?" He pointed to the tall peaks in the distance.

Lily nodded.

"When they gather and turn dark, it usually means rain or snow. This time of year it's snow."

She looked up at him with a curious expression, but Liam saw wisdom and curiosity in her young eyes. He suspected the girl had Miss Abbott to thank, in part, for a decent education. He wished he'd received the same in his orphanage.

"You can tell what's going to happen because of the clouds?"

"Sure can, but we generally get lots of snow this time of year. Christmas doesn't quite feel the same without it."

He'd touched a raw nerve. He could see the flash of pain on Lily's face. "I thought I'd head out and get a tree before it gets dark." Liam glanced once more up at the sky. If he left now, he could cut a nice tree and be back before the sun goes down.

"Can I help?"

"May I help."

Liam and Lily turned at the sound of Miss Abbott's voice from behind them. He hadn't heard the door open, but Lily didn't seem surprised to see her teacher there.

Lily faced him. "May I help?"

Liam nodded. "If it's all right with Miss Abbott."

"It's fine. Go and put on an extra pair of socks and get my gloves. They're on my bed and much warmer for finding Christmas trees."

Lily hesitated for only a few seconds, grinned, and raced off to do as instructed.

Miss Abbott stepped to the railing and gazed out over the snow-covered land and mountains. Liam vividly remembered what it was like his first days on the ranch, in this place so different from the grimy city streets on which he'd first lived.

"Miss Abbott—"

"Please, it's Rebecca."

Liam leaned against the post behind him. "Then call me Liam. I want to assure you that she'll be safe. We won't go far—just to those trees." Liam pointed to the woods at the far edge of his western pasture.

"If I had any worries, they were subdued by Ida. She's quite a force."

Liam laughed. "She is, and she knows it."

Rebecca appeared to sober and finally faced him. Her big amber-tinted eyes looked up at him. "Why have you done this, Liam, really?"

"I figured you would have asked Ida."

"I did." Rebecca shrugged apologetically. "She said it wasn't her story to tell, but from what little she did say, I got the impression that you were once in a situation similar to Lily's."

Similar? Hardly. Lily may not have much to her name except for a change of clothes—something he would rectify soon—and a sharp mind, but she had Rebecca.

He nodded toward the door. "How long will she be?"

Rebecca exhaled and turned back to the scenery. "Not long."

Lily bounded out of the house and stopped short on the porch. She seemed to take in the scene, and surprised Liam when she narrowed her eyes and studied both adults. "Did you make Miss Abbott sad?"

Fiercely loyal and unafraid when it came to protecting the people she loved. Liam like the kid—a lot—and it had only been a day.

"He did no such thing." Rebecca tightened the scarf around Lily's neck and removed a knit cap from her own coat pocket and slipped it onto Lily's head. "Mind Mr. Cassidy."

Still somewhat uncertain, Lily perused Liam's face once more, and he swore the kid saw through to every secret branded on his soul. He knew the technique well. Without it, he wouldn't have survived the streets long enough to make it west.

"May I pick out the tree?"

Liam nodded. They understood each other, even if it was only the initial curiosity and distrust that people like them shared. Ida might have called him and Lily kindred souls in search of the same thing, but they were at different stages of the journey. Ida always did have a musical way with words.

"You can pick out a big tree. Let's go and saddle up. First time on a horse?"

Lily's eyes opened wide and she nodded. "Do I get to get to ride one alone?"

Liam caught the concern on Rebecca's face, but he smiled to try and ease her worry. "You look strong enough, and I've got a gentle mare that could use a ride."

They walked side by side across the way to the barn. Liam kept looking down at Lily's boots, as worn as her coat, and made a note to ride into town in the morning.

After a surprisingly brief lesson on how to hold the reins and stay in the saddle, Liam and his horse guided Lily and the mare away from the barn with a lead rope. Sunbeams peeked through the clouds, though the rays brought no warmth.

"How long have you known Miss Abbott?"

Lily glanced across the few feet and looked up at him. "Two Christmases."

"You really like Christmas, don't you?"

She shrugged. “I think so.” Lily pointed to the trees. “Do we get to pick one of those?”

Liam corrected, “You get to pick one.”

Lily’s big smile brightened her eyes. She kept her gaze trained on the tall pines, and when Liam helped her down from the mare, Lily made a careful study of every tree. She touched each one within reach, her fingers skimming the cold bark of the larger evergreens before wandering farther into the woods where copses of smaller pines grew.

Liam listened to every step while he pulled his ax from the sheath attached to the horse. He turned and stopped. Lily stood before a tree, twice again her size. Perfectly formed with a dusting of snow glistening on its branches. He walked up beside her. “Is this the one?”

She slowly nodded. “It’s the most beautiful tree. I don’t think we should cut it down.”

Liam bent down on one knee on a carpet of snow and needles. “I thought you liked the idea of having a Christmas tree.”

“If we cut it down, it won’t grow anymore.”

Liam smiled. “True. We don’t have to cut it down if you don’t want to. You had Christmas trees at the orphanage. Those came from the woods, too, just like this one.”

Lily turned her head just enough to focus her eyes on him. “They didn’t let us have a tree.”

Liam’s jaw tightened. Life had been tough enough for him growing up in a children’s home, but at least they’d had a tree, even if it had stood bare in the front hall. To have nothing . . . He shook the thought away and stood. “You’re right, the tree won’t continue to grow, but the tree will be honored to be your first ever Christmas tree and will feel special once it’s decorated.”

Lily thought this over and glanced at him curiously. “I guess that’s okay.”

Liam guided her a few feet away and out of range of his swinging ax. With precision and little effort, he swung over and over until the small tree fell onto a blanket of snow.

Lily stared down at the fallen evergreen in wonderment and sadness, but he continued on with the task of hauling the tree to the horses and tying a rope around the trunk and the other end of the rope to his saddle horn.

"It's going to be all right, Lily. I promise."

She accepted his help back onto the mare. Once settled, and before he could turn away, she placed a small hand wearing too big of a glove, on his arm and looked at him squarely. "I believe you, Mr. Cassidy. I think it will be all right, too." They both knew they were talking about more than just the tree. Lily removed her hand and patiently waited for him to remount.

Liam experienced a moment of uncertainty mixed with awe. A child's faith. Did he have that when he first arrived in this mountainous land? He remembered the anger, the uncertainty, and the fear followed by hard word in order to survive. He'd been lucky when Mr. Cassidy took him in but couldn't recall ever once believing in the kind of faith that this young girl had shown him.

"Call me Liam."

They returned to the ranch with tree in tow. Lily's smile returned when she saw Miss Abbott. Liam noticed the immediate change in the girl. Rebecca and Lily were a family. These two women—one a child with a soul beyond her years, and another full grown yet still wary of the world.

Liam hefted the tree onto his shoulder and carried it into the house, carefully navigating the front door and hall. In the main gathering room, Ida already had the usual crock set upon a heavy cloth. Liam lowered the tree into the crock. Ten minutes later, the tree was supported by rocks and filled a corner of the cozy room. Ida promised Lily that they would bring the tree decorations in from the barn in the morning.

Liam asked to speak with Miss Abbott for a moment, but he paused when Lily sat down on the wood floor and gazed up at the tree. Every few seconds she would reach out to touch the low-lying branches. Liam enjoyed the way Miss Abbott's eyes softened whenever she looked at the girl. They both moved quietly into the hall.

"I need to head back into town at first light, so I won't see either of you until before the noon meal. Is there anything you or Lily need from town?"

"You've given us so much already, and we're both grateful."

Liam had put a roof over their heads and food on the table, but her gratitude didn't sit well with him. He didn't want either of them to feel beholden to him for anything, and opted not to tell her about the items he intended to purchase for Lily. "I shouldn't be gone long, and Ida will be here if you need anything."

"I'm certain we'll get along just fine."

Liam nodded and started for the door.

"Mr. Cassidy?"

"It's Liam."

"Do you happen to know if the school here has a teacher?"

Liam watched her hands grip the fabric of her skirt and wondered if it was him or the situation that was making her nervous. "Same teacher since I came here as a young boy. You looking for another job, Miss Abbott?"

"Again, it's Rebecca, please, and yes." She held herself confidently, yet Liam knew she faced an internal struggle. He knew what it was to work hard, and he respected a person—man or woman—who made his or her own way.

"The teacher doesn't get around too well and can't keep up with the young ones, but the children respect her. I imagine she could use some help. I'd be happy to inquire for you."

Rebecca's gaze darted back to the room where Lily still sat enjoying the beauty of the fresh tree. "If you wouldn't mind the company, may I go with you to town? That is, if Ida—"

"Ida would enjoy having Lily to herself for a few hours." Liam studied Rebecca with an even deeper respect. Most women alone in the world would have found a husband to look after her. Rebecca wasn't proud, and Liam didn't doubt that if he hadn't happened along at the church, she would have found a way to keep Lily safe. He was grateful for whatever drew him to the crowded building that morning, whether it was faith or memories. He wasn't going to fight it. "We'll be leaving early."

"I'll be ready.

Rebecca wrapped the single scarf she owned around her neck twice and lowered the wool hat over her ears. She wished she had something to cover her face. The Colorado winter didn't seem any colder than the frigid winters of New York, at least during the day. Early in the morning, before the sun fully rose above the mountains, Rebecca wondered how any sane human being went outside.

She stood next to one of the beams on the front porch and watched Liam lead the horses and wagon to the front of the house.

"Wouldn't horses be faster?"

Liam glanced up at her and then held out his hand to help her into the wagon. She accepted the offer and climbed up to sit on the narrow bench.

"Not in this weather."

He climbed up next to her and reached beneath the seat. When he produced a small, yet heavy blanket, Rebecca was certain this man was an angel. She wrapped the blanket tightly around her body and thanked him.

"I know how to ride."

He shifted, seeming comfortable with the cold air sneaking through the open flaps of his coat. "You learn how to ride teaching children at the orphanage?"

"No. A long time before then." She didn't want to talk about it—not now. Rebecca had known another way of life before she decided on her present course. Every now and then doubt would creep into her mind, and she would question whether or not she'd done the right thing by leaving home. All it took was one smile from Lily to remind her why she'd made the choice.

"We'll try out the horses another time. It's going to be icy in spots, and I'd as soon not have one of them break a leg." He started the team in motion and nodded back toward the house. "Was Lily all right being left behind?"

"Oh, yes. She's quite fascinated with Ida." Rebecca inhaled deeply and nearly choked in the process.

"Take a few deep and steady breaths and drink plenty of water." Liam produced a canteen and handed it over. "The weather and altitude will take some getting used to, but you'll be fine."

Rebecca clutched the canteen with one hand and held the edges of the blanket together with the other. Normally one to enjoy conversation, she found that watching the scenery was more than enough to occupy her time and thoughts. They were blessed. Of all the places she and Lily might have ended up, how did they get so lucky? Rebecca had heard of and studied such places, even seeing photographs in books, and displayed at city galleries by travelers who had trekked from one coast to the next, returning with souvenirs, trinkets to sell, and images of the great open West.

The unassuming town of Cotter's Gulch came into view almost an hour after they had left the ranch. Rebecca must have been more preoccupied when they first arrived than she realized not to notice that the town was a lovely one, with one long street lined with wood and a few brick buildings. Though modest in scale, it was well-tended and in fairly good repair. What held her interest was the grandness of the scenery. She didn't have to lean back far to see the mountain peaks, for they appeared to fill half the landscape.

"What is the name of the mountain standing above the

rest?"

"Those peaks are part of the Rockies. The taller one there is Quandary Peak. I see the mountain and I know I'm home."

Rebecca watched a few residents walk in and out of buildings, but most of the town remained quiet. "Where is everyone?"

Liam chuckled. "Well, you're looking at them. Most folks stay close to home in the winter. With the orphans arriving yesterday, more than usual came out."

Rebecca watched him sober, and she wondered at the change, but she didn't have long to wait.

"I was surprised to see the orphans come this far. Didn't you stop in the bigger towns and cities along the way?"

"Yes, and half the number were adopted, but some thought there was a need for children out here. Have they not come before?"

Liam nodded. "Once, a long time ago." Liam pulled the team to a stop in front of the mercantile and helped Rebecca down from the wagon. "The school teacher is married to the storekeeper. Not a usual arrangement, but we take what we can get."

He walked beside her into the store and leaned over. "We won't be back in town until after Christmas, so if there's anything you or Lily need, just let me know."

Rebecca looked around, taking in the surprising array of goods available. Her gaze settled on the jars of candy arranged on the counter. "Lily would like a piece of candy. We could sometimes get it in New York, but we didn't have time to stop and look on the journey west." She raised her eyes to meet his, and then thought better of it. Her funds were few, but she could do this for Lily. Instead of asking for the candy, she told him, "I'll look around a bit," and walked to the other side of the store.

Liam watched Rebecca's heavy skirts sway slightly until she stopped in front of a bookcase. All she wanted was a piece of candy for Lily, but then she hadn't asked. He didn't doubt she would pay for the candy on her own, and anything else she or Lily might need, before asking him. Liam could understand her desire not to rely on him, and he also knew trust took time.

"Liam, my boy, wasn't expecting you back so soon."

"I forgot a few things yesterday, Arthur." Liam glanced over his shoulder to be certain Rebecca's attention was focused elsewhere. He leaned in and lowered his voice. "Do you have any girl's boots and coats?"

Arthur gave him the expected skepticism, but then must have noticed Liam looking at Rebecca. "I did hear something about a rancher taking a young girl home from the orphan group yesterday. Was that you?"

Liam nodded. "It's a long story, but fact is I did it."

"Well, then who's the lady? She doesn't look like an orphan."

"She's a teacher who came out with the children. She's staying on here with the girl, Lily, but she's looking for a job at the school. Now I know Charlotte might not need any help, and I'll pay for her salary, but—"

"You'll do no such thing." Arthur motioned for Liam to lean in closer. "Charlotte and I have been talking. She doesn't want to leave the children, but she's plum tired out." Arthur looked around Liam's tall frame. "A real teacher, you say?"

"That's what she says. She'd like to talk to Charlotte."

Arthur grinned and walked to the stairs. Instead of walking up them, he stood at the bottom and called to his wife. She yelled right back and a minute later she ambled down the steps. "What's this fuss about, Arthur?"

"Liam brought you a bona fide school teacher."

Liam laughed and met Rebecca's curious gaze. He indicated for her to come over, and when she stood beside him, he placed a hand gently, and briefly on her back before introducing her. “Miss Rebecca Abbott, this is Arthur and Charlotte Little.”

Charlotte held out her hand, and surprised, Rebecca took it. “It sure is a pleasure to meet you, Miss Abbott. Is it true that you’re a teacher?”

“I am, and a good one if say so myself. I had hoped to help—”

“Oh, child, I don’t need help. I need someone to be the new teacher.” Charlotte linked her arm with Rebecca’s and pulled her away, telling the men they’d be back after a spot of tea and a visit.

Liam grinned and turned back to Arthur. “That was settled easier than I thought it would be.”

Arthur waved his hand in the air and chortled. “Charlotte will have her in school and teaching before the students return.” He leaned against the counter and squinted one eye at Liam. “Is the young lady staying with you?”

“Ida’s taking care of her and Lily. Don’t be worried for her.”

“Oh, I trust you, Liam Cassidy, although it’s time you took a wife. I was thinking about how she’ll get into town every day to teach.”

Liam hadn’t thought that far ahead. His immediate concern was ensuring Lily had a proper Christmas. What came after was still a mystery, but one that seemed to be solving itself faster than he could.

“Winter might be tough, but in the good weather, the ride from town doesn’t take too long. She says she can ride, and I’ll teach her to drive the wagon.”

Liam felt Arthur’s stare before he saw it. “What now?”

“Nothing. Nothing at all.” The storekeeper clapped his hands together. “Now, my Charlotte can talk ’til the day is night, but she’ll hurry along because she knows you’re waiting. What’s this about boots and coats?”

Rebecca was a bit bewildered when she emerged from the back parlor with Charlotte. In the first five minutes they'd—or rather Charlotte—had settled the details. Rebecca would begin teaching when school opened the middle of January. She had hoped that work might begin sooner, but she'd manage to stretch her funds until then. When she'd taught in the city, weather rarely interfered with school days, but she imagined in a place like this, with some children living far outside of town, things would be different.

Liam met her smile with one of his own, and she felt a calm within. Somehow everything would be all right. Rebecca wasn't afraid of hard work, or even a struggle to make a good life for her and Lily, but it was almost Christmas and Liam had promised Lily a good one. She would trust him.

Rebecca looked at the counter but saw no packages. Whatever Liam came to purchase was either already in the wagon or wasn't available. Charlotte walked around the counter and her husband pulled her close. Rebecca envied the embrace and the closeness. Two people, comfortable with the time they'd had together, and still looking forward to however many years still ahead.

"We have ourselves a new teacher." Charlotte kissed her husband's cheek and beamed at Rebecca and Liam.

"Don't I need to be approved by the town?"

"Nonsense. We don't have a mayor or town council. We like to run things quiet here, and Charlotte's been in charge of the school since Liam was a young one. If she says you're the new teacher, that's all we need."

Rebecca marveled at how simple it was—and how right it felt. "Thank you, both."

"It's us who should thank you, my dear." Arthur's smile spread across his weathered face. "You just let us know what we can do for you."

"Well, before we leave, I would like to purchase candy.

Lily has a weakness for it. Perhaps a small bag of that hard, colorful candy there."

"Oh, of course!" Arthur overfilled a brown wrapping fashioned into a cone and handed it to her. When she opened her purse, he pulled the candy back to him. "Your money isn't good here today, Miss Abbott. I insist for what you've done for my Charlotte." He handed her the candies. "You take this back to your little girl, and just promise you'll bring her in for a visit. That's all the payment we need."

Arthur reminded Rebecca of the old candy shop owner who lived down the street from the orphanage in the city. He used to sneak Lily small pieces of licorice when he thought Rebecca wasn't looking. It had been a while since she'd been shown such a simple and genuine kindness, except for Liam and Ida's unexpected generosity.

"Thank you, and I promise. Lily would enjoy visiting."

They said their good-byes and Liam helped her into the wagon. Rebecca noticed the covered boxes in the back of the wagon but said nothing when Liam didn't offer an explanation.

When she had first arrived, Rebecca wondered what type of person would choose to live in such a remote place, away from the bustle and convenience of civilization. She expected a rough sort of people without manners. Now, she realized that although there were a few of the rough type, Liam, Ida, and the Littles chose to live in this place on their own terms and build their own dreams. She admired them all for it and would not disappoint them or herself.

They arrived back at the ranch before snow slowly drifted from the gray sky. Rebecca leaned her head back and closed her eyes, allowing a few flakes to settle on her skin. When she noticed Liam watching her, she righted herself and accepted his help from the wagon.

Lily met them on the front porch. Her excitement at their return warmed Rebecca's heart and chipped away the doubts about whether she'd made the right choice in coming west.

Rebecca handed over the bag of candy, doubling Lily's excitement.

"All for me?"

"Of course. No one else I know likes hard candy as much as you do."

Liam spoke from behind them. "Except maybe Ida."

"I'll go and show her!" Lily hugged Rebecca and darted back into the house.

"It doesn't take much, does it?"

Rebecca looked up at Liam, noticing the large wooden box he carried, still covered. "A child like Lily started out with nothing, so even the little things make a difference. No, it doesn't take much."

Once inside, Liam set the box on the floor in the hall and explained that he had to take care of the wagon and horses and then check on the men and cattle. He promised to return by supper. Rebecca watched him leave and then glanced down at the box before hearing her name called out from the kitchen. She entered the cozy room to find Ida and Lily sharing a piece of candy.

"You'll want to put those candies away before you eat too much and spoil your dinner. The storekeeper, Mr. Little, who has those treats in his lovely store, said he would like to meet you. Perhaps when you start school."

Lily perked up. "Are you going to help the teacher?"

"I'm going to be the teacher." Rebecca explained what had taken place with Charlotte.

"I suspected Charlotte was ready for a change." Ida pushed a stray, gray hair back into the knot at the base of her neck. "You'll do just fine."

"I hope so." Rebecca wasn't certain how the nerves managed to creep up on her. She was confident in her abilities but still unsure how she would manage it. Perhaps there would be a room at the boarding house she could rent during the week. She couldn't impose on Liam to borrow a horse or the wagon every day.

A knock at the door drew everyone's attention. Ida wiped her hands on a towel and shook her head. "No creature in his or her right mind would come out this far with the snow falling." Ida didn't move.

"Should we answer it?"

Ida shook her head and moved to the stove. "Liam will have seen them approach and take care of it. Best not to go checking on such things when you don't know who might be there."

Rebecca waited but not for long. Curiosity propelled her to the small window by the front door. It was the figure on the other side who prompted her to open the door and step into the cold. "Mr. Beadle. Whatever are you doing here?" Liam stood between her and Mr. Beadle, blocking the man's path to the porch. Rebecca didn't believe Liam to be a rude person and wondered what might have prompted him not to invite the man out of the cold.

"Ah, Miss Abbott. I have been making an offer to Mr. Cassidy, but he isn't cooperative. Perhaps you can help."

"Help with what?"

"One of the couples who took in a young boy yesterday finds themselves unable to keep him. They prefer a girl. The boy's strong and can work hard, I'm sure. He'd be a help to you on this ranch."

Rebecca leaned forward. "Who is the boy, Mr. Beadle?"

"Billy."

Liam turned his head to look at her. "You know him?"

Rebecca nodded. "He's a good boy, but . . ."

Liam understood her concern and once again faced Mr. Beadle. "If they can't keep the boy, I'll find a place for him here, but Lily's not leaving."

Lily listened intently at the door, and she didn't like what she heard. She knew Billy. Not really well like a best friend, but she liked him. He used to stand up against some of the bullies at the orphan home. No one ever picked on her because she was Miss Abbott's friend, but sometimes the really young ones got teased. Billy wouldn't let that happen if he was around.

Lily stepped outside, even though it was cold and she forgot to put on her ragged coat. "What will happen to Billy?"

Rebecca rushed to her and hugged her close. Lily always felt safe when Miss Abbott held her, but right now she wasn't scared for her. Billy didn't like change, but he was too shy to tell anyone. He didn't have someone like Miss Abbott to protect him.

Mr. Beadle said, "The family simply changed their minds and now want a girl. I know Mr. Cassidy has taken you in, but this other family is kind and they'll take good care of you."

Lily said a silent prayer for strength and looked up at Miss Abbott. Before she could say anything, Liam stepped closer and spoke. "Why can't both children come here?"

Mr. Beadle sighed and shook his head. "It has been done, but if two children are not related, I do try to put them in separate homes."

"They can't have her." Liam's voice remained low but strong. Lily wanted to hug him.

"I can go to the other family." Lily looked up once more at her teacher and friend. "It's all right, Miss Abbott. Billy will like it here. He never had any family, but I got you." She looked again to Liam. "Can I come visit?"

Lily was strong, but she had a difficult time holding back the tears. Liam kneeled down in front of her. "Do you want to leave?"

What should she say? If she told the truth, then Billy would have to stay with the people who didn't want him or maybe go back to the city. Maybe that meant Amos Ward would take him home and poor Billy would be unhappy. She didn't want to lie, but what about Billy? She made the only choice she could—trust Mr. Cassidy.

Lily slowly and tearfully shook her head, and then Miss Abbott pulled her closer. Lily didn't feel the cold as much anymore.

Liam said, "Who has the boy now?"

Mr. Beadle balked, but after a few seconds—Lily counted—he told Mr. Cassidy what he wanted to know. "The Websters."

Rebecca asked, "Do you know them?"

Liam nodded. "They are good people, but too old to be caring for a child." He thought the Websters felt a girl would be of more help to Mrs. Webster. Liam turned to Mr. Beadle. "Will you give me until tomorrow to work things out? I believe I can come up with a solution to satisfy both you and the Websters."

"Well, tomorrow is Christmas Eve." Mr. Beadle hunched inward, pulling his hat down lower and his coat collar higher.

"I know what tomorrow is."

"Very well."

Liam motioned one of his men over. "I'll come into town tomorrow morning, early. One of my men will ride with your wagon back to town. You shouldn't have traveled out here in this weather."

"Quite right."

Lily pulled away from Rebecca and walked around to the back of the house. Rebecca moved to go after her, but Liam halted her with a gentle touch. "She just needs some time alone." Liam had an idea of what was going on in Lily's mind for he'd been in a similar situation more than twenty years ago. "Mr. Beadle, I'll ride back into town with you as well." He pulled Rebecca aside and spoke softly. "You'll need to get back inside before you're too chilled. I'll try to get back before nightfall, but I may not return until morning."

"What do you have planned? Mr. Beadle can't take Lily from you if that's what's worrying you."

"I'm not worried, and I don't believe it's what Mr. Beadle wants. He's just trying to make the best of a difficult situation." Liam remembered the man who came west with him and the small group of boys and girls, and by comparison, Amos Ward would have been a better choice to look after a child's well-being. He'd been lucky, but many children hadn't, and most of them were not like Lily. He can't think of one of them who would have considering giving up a new home for another orphan.

"I brought the Christmas decorations in from the barn already, but there is another large box of tree ornaments in the attic that Ida has been collecting over the years. She knows where it's at, and I'll have one of the men help bring it down. It should help you occupy Lily because she won't be thinking of much else besides the boy."

"Are you going to speak with the Websters?"

Liam nodded. "I don't know what good it will do, and I can't imagine why they thought to take in a child. Just keep Lily close, and I'll be back as soon as I can. Tomorrow's Christmas Eve, and I don't intend on disappointing Lily."

Liam started to move away, but this time it was Rebecca who stopped him. "I haven't asked, but the crate you brought home from the mercantile . . ."

He'd forgotten. "Have Ida help, but you'll know what to do with everything."

With that cryptic declaration, Liam walked down the steps and told Mr. Beadle to wait for him. Rebecca opened the front door, but her former supervisor's voice halted her.

"You look well, Miss Abbott. I don't wish to cause you or the girl any unhappiness. I can see that Mr. Cassidy was the right choice."

Rebecca turned and let the door close with a soft click. "Then why did you come here today? Why not simply tell the Websters that there are no other children?"

"I didn't do it for them, Miss Abbott. I did it for the boy. They can provide for him, but because they don't want a boy, they may never give him the love he needs."

Rebecca studied the man carefully, surprised by his confession. She rubbed her hands up and down her arms, hugging herself against the cold, but she remained outside on the porch. Mr. Beadle was not the cold-hearted administrator she had once believed him to be. He truly seemed to care for the children. Would she have been able to make different decisions had the responsibility of the orphans been left to her?

"You won't try to take Lily away?"

"No, I won't."

Rebecca felt relief and guilt all at once. "Mr. Beadle, your kindness does you credit." She then fell silent until Liam appeared with his horse. Once Mr. Beadle was in the wagon, Liam tied his Appaloosa to the back and joined the other man on the buckboard, taking the reins in hand. Without another good-bye, he set the horses in motion and rode into the light snow.

Rebecca exhaled the breath she'd been holding and called out for Lily. Once. Twice. Lily didn't respond, nor did she return. Clad in only her wool dress and thin boots, she followed Lily's footsteps in the snow. The girl had walked around to the back of the house, and it was there, on a frost-covered bench beside a dormant garden, where Rebecca found her. She ran through the snow as best she could and enveloped Lily in her arms.

"It's far too cold for either of us to be out here, Lily." She lifted the girl's chin until she could look into her damp eyes. "Whatever is wrong? You won't be taken away, I promise." And she knew with Liam's help, that's a promise she could keep.

"Billy."

"Dear girl, Billy will be all right."

"I don't think so, Miss Abbott. Billy said not all of us would get families, and maybe if we did, the family wouldn't like us." Lily bit on her lower lip and trembled.

“Come inside now, before we both freeze.” Rebecca hurried the girl into the house through the back door, which led into the kitchen. When Ida saw them both pale and covered in a dusting of snowflakes, she ushered them to sit beside the fire.

“Whatever possessed you two to go out there without proper clothes?” Ida opened the door to a small storeroom and emerged with two quilts. “You just sit there and get warm while I fix you a bit of tea.”

Ida fixed the tea, a cup of cocoa for Lily, and fussed with the fire until both of them had a little color back in their cheeks. “Now, tell me what this is all about.”

Liam climbed down from his horse, the cold night air not slowing his movements. He helped his guest down to the ground and coaxed him into the house. Laughter and music greeted them before the front door even opened. Liam hadn’t known what his life had been missing until now.

He hung their coats just inside the front door and walked quietly to the entrance of the main gathering room in the house. There in the corner stood the tall evergreen Lily had picked out, covered now in candles, ribbon, and an assortment of glass balls Ida had ordered from the East. The laughter seemed to have something to do with Rebecca’s current position on the floor with her arms and legs flung out and an angel held high in one hand.

“Do you need some help?”

Rebecca floundered, attempting to right herself, but Lily continued to giggle even as she held out her hand. Instead of waiting for the inevitable fall that would occur when Lily tried to pull up her teacher, Liam hurried over and gently raised Rebecca off the floor. She righted her skirts and looked up in time to catch his smile.

“We were just trying to—.”

“I see that.” Liam turned and motioned the boy forward. “It seems we’ve arrived just in time.”

"Billy!" Lily rushed forward, and with a child's affection, embraced her friend.

"Billy is staying for Christmas."

Liam watched Lily pluck the angel from Rebecca's hand and pull her friend to the tree, and then ask Billy, "Do you want to put the angel on top?"

Billy looked down at Lily and then over to Liam for permission. Liam nodded, and then held the small ladder steady while the boy climbed up and set the angel at the top. The children stood back to admire their work when Ida stepped in and announced that the first batch of jumbles, or spiced butter cookies. With Rebecca's permission, they followed Ida back to the kitchen.

Rebecca walked up beside Liam while he put the ladder in the hall. "However did you manage to bring him here?"

Liam responded with a question of his own. "Did you really fall off this ladder? You could be hurt and not realize it."

"I assure you that only my pride is bruised. I managed the steps quite well until last time. I tripped on the bottom rung, so the fall was not great."

Liam's gaze moved from her rumpled skirt up to her hair, which she obviously didn't know was still in disarray. He enjoyed seeing her like this—not entirely proper—but still quite beautiful. He walked toward the kitchen, indicating for Rebecca to follow. His eyes fixed on Lily and Billy who were presently enthralled by an old Irish Christmas tale Ida was spinning.

Liam kept his voice low so as not to disturb the others. "I stopped off at the Websters' on the way home. It turns out Mr. Beadle misunderstood their wishes. They originally wanted a boy to help tend their small gardens and the few animals they have left. However, two of their own children arrived as a Christmas surprise. Turns out they came to take their parents back east with them. Mrs. Webster thought it would be nice to have a young girl act as her companion on the journey, but she never meant for Mr. Beadle to try and take Lily away."

"What would they have done with Billy had you not come by?"

"Give him back to Mr. Beadle, I suppose. He should do well here."

"You're keeping him?"

Liam studied Rebecca's wide eyes and knew it would be a while yet before she wasn't surprised by simple acts of kindness. He remembered that feeling—not knowing who to trust or accepting generosity when it was unexpected. Had it not been for Roane Cassidy, Liam could have spent most of his life on the edge, without compassion for others.

"Billy's strong, and ranching is a good trade to learn. He could do worse than here. Besides, I don't think Lily would let me send him away." Liam watched the young girl and boy, only a few years apart in age, their hands linked. "She talked about Billy protecting the younger children at the orphan home, but it's Lily watching out for him now."

"She would have given up this home, this chance, for him."

Liam nodded, an overwhelming hope and peace filling his heart. "I know."

Rebecca gently rested her hand on his arm. "Thank you, Liam."

Liam lowered his eyes and fixed onto hers. He understood the internal pull toward this gentle and caring woman who had brought light and joy into his home. They would have time—plenty of time if Liam had his way—to know how their futures would intertwine. For now, he was in awe of his good fortune and sent up a silent "thank you" to Roane Cassidy for not turning him away. When others had given up on a young boy from the city, Roane had taught him the importance of love and family.

Ida ambled over, drawing Liam's gaze away from Rebecca. "I think it's time for some of that special cake I've been saving."

Surprised, Liam grinned. "You never let me anywhere near that Christmas cake of yours before the day comes."

"I'll make pie for Christmas dinner this year." Ida looked over at the children, who now sat in front of the fire, staring up at the tree. "Tonight's a true celebration."

"We have to be quiet." Lily hunched low as she walked on her toes along the upstairs hall and down the stairs. She stopped and Billy ran into her from behind. "Careful, Billy."

"Why do we have to be quiet?"

"We're trying to see Santa. Liam said he always comes to Cotter's Gulch, but no one has ever seen him before."

Billy sighed. "Santa isn't real, Lily. If he was, he would have come to the orphanage."

Lily waved the idea away. "Maybe he just doesn't like cities." She waited another moment and grinned. "All right, I think everyone else is still asleep."

"Like we should be." Billy grumbled a little, but his curiosity drove him to follow Lily. They reached the doorway to the gathering room where the fireplace flames still burned. The candles on the tree had been blown out before they all went to bed, but the flames flickered, causing shadows to dance on the walls. "I don't see anyone."

"Shh." Lily inched forward and peeked around the corner until she saw the tree. "He's not here." She stepped into the room, her eyes growing wide. "Billy, look!"

Billy walked around her and looked where she pointed. Beneath the tree sat four bundles wrapped in fabric and paper.

"What do you think they are?"

"I don't know." She closed the distance to the tree and knelt beside one of the bundles. "Have you ever seen anything so grand?"

Billy shook his head. "Santa must have known you were here."

“You, too. I bet one of these is for you.”

“Nah, Santa didn’t know where to find me, but that’s okay.” Billy reached out to touch one, but then pulled his hand back. “You ever get a Christmas present before?”

Lily almost said “no,” but she paused. She looked around her at the cozy room and the big tree Liam let her pick out. Her eyes looked up at the ceiling where she knew in the rooms above slept Liam, Ida, and Rebecca. Lily then looked over at Billy, his light blond hair almost glowing in the firelight. “Not until now.”

Dear, God. Thank you for giving me a family. Merry Christmas. Love, Lily.

The End

The Wycliffe Hotel's Famous Coffee Cake Recipe

As featured in *Teton Christmas*

Note that this recipe has been adapted for use in modern-day kitchens.

Ingredients

2 1/3 cups all-purpose flour
¾ cup unsalted butter, softened
1 cup coconut flakes
½ cup brown sugar
1 teaspoon ground cinnamon
2 ½ teaspoons baking powder
½ teaspoon sea salt
1 cup granulated sugar
2 whole eggs
2 cup non-fat milk
2 ½ cup fresh berries (equal parts of huckleberry, blackberry, and raspberry)*
*You may also use any one of the berries listed rather than a combination.

Directions

1. Combine 1/3 cup flour, ¼ cup butter, the coconut, brown sugar, and cinnamon. Mix until crumbly and set aside.
2. Preheat oven to 375 degrees F and prepare a 13" baking pan using a non-stick baking spray. You may also use shortening and flour.

3. Sift remaining 2 cups flour with the baking powder and salt, into a small bowl.
4. Beat remaining ½ cup butter until fluffy.
5. Gradually add 1 cup sugar, beating until well blended.
6. Add eggs one at a time, beating after each addition.
7. Mix dry ingredients into batter, alternating with the milk, in three additions.
8. Gently fold in the berries.
9. Transfer the thick mixture from the bowl to the prepared pan.
10. Sprinkle evenly with the coconut topping.
11. Bake at 375 degrees F for approximately 45 minutes or until done. If you're uncertain how your oven bakes, check the cake after 35 minutes.

Happy Holidays from Caitlyn Marsh, proprietor of the Wycliffe Hotel.

Find more of MK's favorite recipes at www.mkmcclintock.com

ABOUT THE AUTHOR

MK McClintock is an author, entrepreneur, and photographer. She enjoys spending hours walking along rivers or over mountains, loves the Scottish Highlands, and likes to put her creative energy to use in the kitchen. With her heart deeply rooted in the past, and her mind always on adventure, she lives and writes in Montana.

Learn more about MK by visiting her website: http://www.mkmcclintock.com.

Interested in reading more by MK McClintock? Try her Montana Gallagher novels—stories about family, hope, love, and justice in nineteenth-century Montana territory.

The Montana Gallagher series:
Book One – *Gallagher's Pride*
Book Two – *Gallagher's Hope*
Book Three – *Gallagher's Choice*

You may also try her British Agent Novels, stories of mystery, adventure, and romance set in the Victorian British Isles.

The British Agent Novels:
Book One – *Alaina Claiborne*
Book Two – *Blackwood Crossing*
Book Three – *Clayton's Honor* (coming 2015)